KW-621-045

SMILE OF THE TIGER

SMILE OF THE TIGER

Caroline Charles

CHIVERS
THORNDIKE

This Large Print book is published by BBC Audiobooks Ltd, Bath, England and by Thorndike Press®, Waterville, Maine, USA.

Published in 2006 in the U.K. by arrangement with the author

Published in 2006 in the U.S. by arrangement with Juliet Burton Literary Agency

U.K. Hardcover ISBN 1–4056–3781–1 (Chivers Large Print)
ISBN 13: 978 1 405 63781 7
U.K. Softcover ISBN 1–4056–3782–X (Camden Large Print)
ISBN 13: 978 1 405 63782 4
U.S. Softcover ISBN 0–7862–8736–5 (British Favorites)

Copyright © Caroline Charles, 1986

All rights reserved.

The text of this Large Print edition is unabridged.
Other aspects of the book may vary from the original edition.

Set in 16 pt. New Times Roman.

Printed in Great Britain on acid-free paper.

British Library Cataloguing in Publication Data available

Library of Congress Cataloging-in-Publication Data

Charles, Caroline.
Smile of the tiger / by Caroline Charles.
p. cm.
"Thorndike Press large print British favorites."
ISBN 0–7862–8736–5 (pbk. : alk. paper)
1. Businessmen—Fiction. 2. Triangles (Interpersonal relations)—Fiction. 3. Large type books. I. Title.
PR6053.H3717S65 2006
813'.54—dc22 2006010068

KIRKLEES CULTURE AND LEISURE SERVICES

ACC NO.	351 608 244
CLASS NO	
Order No	CUL 32962 / 129303
Date	8.11.06
Price	£15.99
Supplier	BBC
Loc	

CHAPTER ONE

That leap year day, February twenty-ninth, had been a busy one for Christiana. The last thing she needed was to have to get dressed up for an American businessman who was coming to dinner. Should she pin her hair up, or leave it loose?

A sharp tap on the door preceded her mother's, 'Hurry up, Chris. He's here.'

'Coming!' she called, and decided she had better put her hair up, after all. Sighing, she sat down at her dressing table and reached for her hair pins. All this fuss for some stranger whom she visualised as middle-aged, silver-haired, wearing steel-rimmed glasses, speaking with a nasal twang and probably possessing little sense of humour. Even his name was awful—Jason Straker.

Not for the first time, she wondered if she was making a mistake by remaining at home in Yorkshire instead of striking out independently, but she loved the big old house where she had grown up, she had a good relationship with her parents, and she could still follow her career. She even had her own studio.

A final glance in the mirror, a hair removed from her black velvet skirt, and she told herself she would suffice. She walked unhurriedly down the carpeted corridor and the stairway which angled down to a long, parquet-floored hallway. A murmur of voices drew her to the sitting-room.

Her mother rose to her feet with an alacrity that told Christiana she was nervous. 'Chris, where have you been?'

'Sorry,' Christiana apologised. 'Last minute snags.'

Then she saw the man who had risen from the settee beside her father. She hoped she didn't look as stunned as she felt.

'My daughter Christiana,' her father was saying as her hand became enveloped in the big, warm hand of Jason Straker and green eyes smiled at her from a tanned face. He was well over six feet tall, much younger than she had expected, and masculine to his fingertips.

'Miss Deverill,' he drawled, inclining his head slightly and smiling so that his cheeks indented in the most disarming manner.

'How do you do?' she replied, being if anything a touch too cool and formal.

'You're a designer,' he remarked, green eyes still smiling. 'Fashion?'

Christiana gave a deprecatory laugh. 'Nothing so glamorous, I'm afraid. Fabrics and wallpaper.'

'She paints, too,' her father put in, and to Christiana's embarrassment, he drew Mr Straker's attention to the portraits either side of the chimney breast, one of himself, one of his wife.

'They're very good,' the guest commented on cue, but he slid a sidelong glance at Christiana that made her wonder if he was laughing at her.

Her father supplied drinks and smalltalk ensued. Christiana added her share to the conversation, but she found it hard not to keep staring at Jason Straker.

Other guests began to arrive, departmental managers and their wives coming to meet the new partner at Deverill's. The party swelled to twelve, including Brian Fleming, the clever young head of accounts who had brought his pretty sister along. Christiana had always liked Beth Fleming, but when she saw her light up in front of Jason Straker, and saw him respond with flirtatious warmth, she bridled a little.

'Charmer, isn't he?' Brian murmured beside her. 'But you know what they say about the smile on the face of the tiger; what lies behind this deal, I wonder? The thickening wedge? American takeover?'

'You're just naturally suspicious,' she told him. 'My father's delighted about it all. And Beth doesn't seem to have any qualms.'

'Beth's just an impressionable woman.'

'You really don't like women much, do you?' Christiana observed.

'Oh, I wouldn't say that.' He gave her the full attention of his steady grey eyes. 'But it would take a very special girl to make me give up any of my interests and you're not about to reciprocate, are you?'

Surprise made Christiana stare at him, and after a split second Brian looked away, saying, 'Sorry. Just testing the temperature of the water. Forget it . . .'

Christiana's work took her to London for a week to obtain some samples of fabric and to discuss the basic colours which would predominate during next season.

When she returned to Arnside House she found the Yorkshire dales heady with the promise of spring. The countryside bloomed with pale green in all the trees and hedges, and daffodils bobbed their golden heads.

As she walked along the hallway, her mother emerged from her sewing-room to say, 'Thank goodness you're home. Have you forgotten the Mayor's Ball is tonight?'

'I shan't be going,' Christiana replied. 'I thought I'd told you that; I hate those stuffy, formal functions. Don't worry about me, I'm buzzing with ideas that I want to get started on.'

'But you've got to come!' her mother exclaimed. 'Otherwise Mr Straker won't have a partner. Your father promised him you'd be there.'

Wondering why her pulses had suddenly jumped, Christiana said, 'I'm sure Mr Straker's quite capable of finding his own partner.'

'You can't let your father down,' Mrs

Deverill pleaded. 'It's important, Chris. Mr Straker needs to meet people socially. Poor man, he's still living in that hotel, trying to find somewhere suitable to live. What chance has he had to find a lady friend yet? Please, do it for us . . .'

'Oh, all right,' Christiana replied ungraciously.

The prospect of spending an evening as Jason Straker's partner was deliciously enticing, as Christiana discovered while she bathed and dressed. She found herself taking special care with her make-up and grooming, but she hoped he wouldn't think that her off-the-shoulder gown of midnight blue had been chosen merely for his pleasure.

The cream of Medfordham society gathered at the Assembly Rooms, laughter and conversation swelling as the tables around the dance-floor filled with people. Waiters flitted around and the dancing began.

Of Jason Straker, to Christiana's annoyance, there was no sign.

After a while, the quick-steps and waltzes gave way to a disco beat and Christiana was asked to dance by Brian Fleming. She threw herself into the beat, improvising steps, but for some reason she was aware of the exact moment when Jason Straker walked in to join her parents. Was it more than exertion that made her breathless?

When eventually Brian led her back to the

table, Jason Straker rose to his feet, his bland smile teasing her. Her senses jumped as she realised she had forgotten how compelling he was in the flesh, especially in that black dinner jacket and snowy shirt, across which flecks of coloured light flitted.

'I'm sorry I was delayed,' he said smoothly. 'You look beautiful, Miss Deverill. Hi, Brian, how goes it?'

'Good evening, Mr Straker,' Brian returned stiffly. 'Nice to see you. I'll, er, see you later, Christiana.'

'Fine,' she replied with a too-bright smile.

'Mr Straker had to wait in for a phone call from the States,' her mother was saying as Christiana took her seat.

'I'm afraid so,' Jason said, his thoughts hidden behind that maddening smile. 'I hope I'm forgiven. If I'd known . . .' But his excuses were drowned by an eruption of music as the room once more vibrated with sound.

Her parents decided to try a step or two, leaving Christiana alone with the man whose very presence had all her nerves on the alert. Having glanced at the seething throng, Jason shrugged as if to say that talking was impossible. That slow, knowing smile lit his face, making his eyes dance with devilment.

He took a notebook and gold pen from an inner pocket and jotted down a few words before turning the page for her to see. *Too crowded,* he had written. *Later?*

He slid the notebook along the table, the pen on top of it, gesturing her to follow his lead.

Pursing her lips, she wrote, *If you like*, which made him slant a reproving eyebrow at her and add a few more words, which read, *I do like. How about you?*

Are we talking about dancing? she enquired on the page, watching with mock innocence as he laughed to himself and responded, *Only for the moment.*

Eventually the band swung into a slow foxtrot which made Jason say, 'That's more like it. Shall we?' He led her on to the dance floor and took her in his arms, sweeping her with fluid ease into the steps. 'Relax,' he ordered under his breath.

'I am.'

'Liar. Come here, it'll be easier.' The arm around her waist tightened, pulling her against him. Now she could feel the flow of his muscles as his thighs brushed hers and their feet moved in unison.

One tune changed to another, and then a third. Only when the last note faded did he stop and allow her out of his arms, smiling at her flushed face.

'Thank you,' Christiana said brightly, pretending it had been just a dance like any other.

'My pleasure,' he replied.

A buffet supper had been set up in another room and Mr Deverill suggested he and Jason might fetch plates for all of them, to save the ladies being caught in the crush.

'Now, aren't you glad you came?' her mother said, watching Jason's departing figure with soft eyes. 'What a lovely man! If I were your age, and single, I'd be over the moon.'

'I agree, Mr Straker has a way with him, but what do we know about him? He blows in here, takes over half the firm and—'

'Oh, your father knows what he's doing. The connection with Strakers in the States is very useful.'

'I understand Jason had taken the partnership on his own account?'

'So he has, but his family own a similar business in . . . I think it's Milwaukee. He knows the engineering business inside out, but he wanted to strike out on his own. And from our point of view the extra capital is welcome. There's also the point that a younger man will be able to take over when your father retires.'

Before she could prevent herself, Christiana heard herself ask, 'Do you know whether Jason's married?'

Her mother blinked. 'Oh, I don't think so. He doesn't behave like a married man.'

'Which means exactly nothing,' replied her more cynical daughter. 'After all, he must be—what? Thirty-four or so?'

'He's probably just waiting for the right girl.' Mrs Deverill smiled. 'Like you, waiting for Mr Right. Wouldn't it be wonderful if the two of you turned out to be just the right ones for each other?'

'It would be a miracle,' Christiana said.

After supper, she found herself accompanying Jason across the lobby to a bar where he chose a corner table and ordered fresh drinks.

'We can talk better here,' he said, taking a seat opposite her. He looked at her, surveying her creamy shoulders lazily. 'Sure you're warm enough?' he asked.

'I'm fine, thank you.' She sipped her drink, casting around for some neutral subject to talk about. 'Have you been in England long?'

'Around three weeks, this trip. You travel much?'

'A little, mostly on business. I'm going to an exhibition in Brussels next month.'

'Quite the cosmopolitan lady, eh?'

'Oh, quite!' She laughed, to show that she didn't take herself too seriously.

'How come you don't have a boy friend?' he asked.

'Who said I don't?' she countered, suddenly wary.

'Your father.'

Christiana widened her eyes mockingly. 'Mr Straker, have you been making enquiries about me?'

'Nope. He dropped it into the conversation. You've got friends of both sexes, but no one special right now.'

'How very boring of my father to mention it,' she murmured drily. 'As if you'd be in the least interested.'

'Well, naturally I am,' he bantered. 'You're a beautiful girl, Chrissy. So what's wrong?'

That personal stab made her sit up, saying coolly, 'Nothing that I'm aware of. And please don't call me Chrissy.'

'Why not?'

'Because I don't like it.' She stood up, disturbed by the trend of the conversation. 'Isn't it time we were going back to the ballroom?'

'Sure,' he agreed, languidly leaving his seat to stand close beside her, a hand lightly at her waist as he added, 'I can't wait to dance some more with you, either.'

Although she maintained her cool poise for the rest of the evening, reliving it all later she had to laugh to herself. He had teased her relentlessly, chipping away at her armour. Now, in the darkness of night, that dreadful, tantalising, fascinating man insinuated himself into dreams in which she no longer behaved like a prickly English rose but like the woman she really was.

She fully expected him to call her within a day or two, though as she told herself afterwards, she hadn't the least desire to see him again.

But the days went by and he didn't call—and that bothered her . . .

CHAPTER TWO

At Easter, a charity exhibition and auction were held in Arndale. The exhibits were on show in a converted barn where one low-beamed room led to another via stairs and passageways. Having given two of her own paintings to help the cause, Christiana went along on the day of the auction and spent some time admiring the work of local artists and craftsmen.

Wearing a pink suit of lacy wool, with a matching hat, broad-brimmed and set low on her brow, she paused to study a beautifully worked tapestry picture and decided she would bid for it when the sale began.

'Well, hello,' came a soft, deep voice beside her, making her heart skip a beat as Jason Straker bent to peer under her hat. 'Mata Hari? Greta Garbo? No—it's you, Chrissy.'

She sighed in annoyance, denying the jump of her senses. 'I've asked you not to call me that.'

'There I go again,' he said, green eyes dancing. 'Sorry, Miss Deverill.' Her hat seemed to fascinate him. 'That's an eye-catcher. Literally.'

'Then keep your distance,' Christiana suggested with a narrow smile.

'Is that what it's for—'protective clothing?'

His grin made dimples in his cheeks, so that she laughed with him.

'You like that picture?' he asked, nodding at the tapestry.

'It's wonderful. All those tiny stitches, so that every detail's clear—the millwheels, the flowers, even the cat catching birds, it must have taken hours of work.'

She moved on, Jason beside her. Her own pictures were next on the wall. She would have walked past, but Jason stepped in front of her to examine the paintings, one of autumn woods and horses, the other an imaginary scene of moonlight on a lake.

'C. Deverill,' he read the name inscribed at the foot of each picture, and glanced at her in surprise. 'I'd never have guessed you were a romantic.'

Christiana allowed herself an enigmatic smile. 'I wouldn't assume too much, if I were you.'

As she turned her head away, he leaned across to look at her face. 'An artist reveals his soul in his work.'

'How profound,' Christiana snapped at him.

'You'd argue with that?' he said curiously. 'You mean you're really like this, all through?'

She shot him a glance from her eye corner. 'Like what?'

'Deep frozen.'

Now that, she thought, was below the belt. She gave him a flashing glance that ought to have shrivelled him, and at that moment a bell rang to signal the start of the auction.

In the general crush to get to the main room of the building, Christiana managed to evade Jason Straker, though as the auction got under way she remained pricklingly aware of his presence across the room.

To her surprise, when her picture of the moonlit lake came up for sale, Jason determinedly bid for it. He eventually bought the picture by upping the price well ahead of his competitors, which caused several people to glance at Christiana and smile, not so much in congratulation as in curiosity, she thought. Hadn't Jason heard of discretion?

The tapestry picture of the old rustic mill soon came under the hammer and at first several people, including Christiana, put in bids. At twenty pounds the picture was about to go to Christiana when Jason's voice chimed in, 'And five.' He carried on bidding up to fifty pounds.

As soon as she could, she escaped while everyone else was talking and discussing the success of the sale. But as she hurried across the car park to her old banger, a familiar voice hailed her. 'Hey, Chrissy! Hold it a minute. I've got something for you,' he said, arriving beside her as she approached her car.

He slid in beside the car so that she couldn't open the door, and she saw he was carrying his acquisitions—her painting under one arm, the tapestry picture in his other hand. 'This is for you.'

'Well, I don't want it,' she said, backing away because he was much too close. 'I couldn't possibly accept such an expensive gift from a stranger.'

He stopped trying to give her the picture and his frown darkened. 'You think I'm just a pushy Yank, don't you?'

'Oh, I wouldn't say that,' she replied in a sweetly acid voice.

'No, I guessed you wouldn't,' he returned with disgust. 'You wouldn't have the guts to be that honest.'

As he moved away from the car, she wrenched open the door, threw herself in, and drove off without so much as looking in his direction.

* * *

April drifted into May. Though Christiana heard plenty about Jason Straker from her father and from Brian Fleming, whom she encountered once or twice while playing badminton at the local sports centre, she didn't set eyes on him.

Her trip to Brussels to a design exhibition, went very well. She travelled to London a couple of times, and in between worked hard at her studio.

On a blazing day at the end of May, she and

her mother drove down the dale to watch a charity cricket match. Brian Fleming was playing, along with several other members of the Deverill workforce, and Mr Deverill had been asked to umpire.

Christiana and her mother set up deckchairs well in the shade of swaying, leafy branches, relaxing as the match progressed. Mr Deverill joined them for a picnic lunch and then the match resumed. It was a leisurely game.

'Is there any more tea?' her mother asked.

' 'Fraid not.' She yawned. 'I'll get you some, though. There's a kiosk near the gate.'

She set off through the trees, stepping over fallen branches and pushing through undergrowth until she reached the track which led to the gate, where a wooden kiosk sold sweets, ices and drinks. Unfortunately, the tea was very hot, so that carrying it was tricky. Christiana decided not to risk the woods, but went instead down the track, behind scattered parties of spectators.

Since her eyes were fixed on the level of the tea, she failed to see the long legs sprawled among knee-high grass until she tripped and almost fell. The tea splashed, scalding hot on her hands, as the man leapt up and relieved her of the cups. Only then did she realise it was Jason Straker.

'You all right?' he asked.

'I'm fine.' She gritted her teeth, wiping her wet hands on her jeans.

'I guess I was half-asleep. I'm sorry. Let me carry these for you.'

He seemed genuinely contrite, though she had no intention of letting that soften her.

'Mother's along here,' she muttered, leading the way, part of her exultant at being with him, the rest of her in turmoil.

Mrs Deverill seemed delighted to see Jason and offered him a rather warm squash, which he took. He drank it from the can, sitting on the grass on the far side of Mrs Deverill while Christiana resumed her own seat and pretended utter indifference. Eventually, however, she excused herself.

Feeling thoroughly out of sorts with the world and with herself, she stalked away, making down a path that twisted deep into the woods, running downhill until it emerged in a sunny glade surrounded by greenery, where a stream rippled cold and clear over rounded stones. Faintly she could hear the occasional clatter of applause from the cricket field, but here in the glade there was only the stream rippling, the breeze moving among leaves, birds calling, and a high veil of cloud like a chiffon scarf drifting across the blue sky.

She leaned against a tree, staring moodily at the stream.

Some sixth sense told her she was not alone. She whirled away from the tree and saw Jason watching her with a set face. He had his fists stuffed into the pockets of his slacks and his shirt was open to reveal a bronzed torso enhanced by dark hairs.

Her hands clenched tight at her sides as she drew herself up and demanded, 'Are you following me?'

'No, I'm hunting elephant,' he retorted. 'What do you think I'm doing? Of course I followed you!'

Christiana tossed her head. 'Then you can just take yourself away again!'

He started towards her, but she backed away.

'Don't touch me!' Suddenly she was terrified, not so much of him as of her own reactions if he got too near.

She gasped as his strong hands clamped on her shoulders. She froze with shock, clamping her lips shut as his mouth came down on hers. This wasn't how she wanted it to be. Not like this! She would have fought him, but his arms had locked round her, pinioning her arms to her sides. He bent her backward, punishing her with a savage kiss that left her breathless with despair and outrage.

After a moment he held her away from him, his lip curling in scorn as he stared down at her furious eyes. 'Just as I thought—arctic.'

A wave of rage mounted inside her, fuelled by the knowledge that she was close to tears. She was human enough to be wounded by his inferences that she was frigid, and her temper abruptly came up with what seemed an ideal way of exacting revenge.

Keeping her gaze locked with his, she said, evenly, 'You think I'm frigid, do you, Mr Straker?' She rested a forefinger on his chest, drawing slow circles through the hairs that curled there.

His expression changed from scorn to wariness, but she noted the stiffening of his muscles and the indrawn breath he took in response to her stroking finger.

'You think I'm cold?' she enquired hoarsely, hating herself for what she was doing but feeling that he deserved it. She let her hand slide sensuously up his chest to curl behind his neck. She reached up and kissed him full on the mouth, her lips soft and coaxing, moving on his. After a moment's hesitation when she could sense his struggle with himself, Jason's mouth parted in unwilling but undeniable response.

She was caught in her own trap and her senses began to respond to the warmth of him pressed so close she could feel every muscle.

He lifted his head, his pupils wide in blazing eyes that held a bewildered astonishment that matched her own. For long moments their eyes asked silent questions. Is it true? Is it really happening? For you, too? Then he bent to taste her mouth again and this time she responded without reserve, letting her fingers twist and knead in his hair.

Fighting it was useless, she knew. Despite

her resistance, her soul had been invaded, taken over, and nothing in the world could have stopped it.

But something did stop it.

'I've got to tell you.' Jason groaned. 'Chrissy, I'm engaged to be married.'

She couldn't move. She was paralysed by disbelief. What had he said? All at once the heat left her and she was aware of the breeze and the birds in the trees. He couldn't be engaged to someone else; he belonged to her! It was written in the stars. Wasn't it?

Jason's face twisted with remorse. He jerked away from her. 'I'm sorry.' Now she was aware of the cool breeze on her skin, and of her shame. 'Sorry?' she croaked.

He turned to look at her with the eyes of a stranger. Even his voice didn't sound like his own as he said, 'You shouldn't have tempted me, Chris.'

Unable to stand the sight of him any longer, she turned and fled away from the unbearable memories in that glade, not knowing where she was going, not caring. Somehow she had to get away from the searing pain of betrayal. She had given more of herself to him than she had ever given to any man, and he could do this to her!

She was scarcely aware of the tears of grief that streamed down her face.

CHAPTER THREE

Several days later, Christiana was in the study which had become her refuge, her drawing board covered in ideas for designs which somehow wouldn't come right. She had tried everything she knew to break the block on her inspiration, but nothing helped.

The studio lay at the side of the house, connected to the main building by a corridor. She had a marvellous view over the gardens bright with early summer, sloping down to the river Arn with the sweep of hills in the distance. But Yorkshire seemed to have lost its appeal.

Across the expanse of the big, bare-floored room, the door opened and Christiana swung round, her head tightening as she saw Jason come in, wearing a business suit. In one hand he carried the straw hat which had fallen from her during their encounter in the glade.

'Who let you in here?' she demanded coldly.

He closed the door, leaned on it, head on one side as he watched her with sombre eyes. The sight of him made her heart ache even while she told herself again that she hated him.

'Your mother told me where to find you,' he said. 'What else was I supposed to do? I call, and you won't talk to me. I wrote you a letter, but you didn't reply.'

'Because there's nothing at all that I have to say to you!' she replied, turning to the tall swivel stool behind her drawing board. 'Please go away. I'm busy.'

Picking up a piece of charcoal, she took a fresh piece of paper and began to draw in sweeping, angry strokes, ignoring Jason as he came slowly across the room, his shoes sounding heavy on the bare floor.

He lunged to stop the movement. 'Please!' The charcoal scored across the paper. 'You must listen to me!'

Tearing her hand away from the unbearable touch of his, she jumped from her seat. 'There's no "must" about it. I don't want to hear your excuses, Mr Straker.'

'Christiana . . .' His hesitation seemed to last an age. 'I never meant . . . Believe me, I didn't realise what was happening, until it was too late.'

'You didn't realise,' she said flatly, glancing at him over her shoulder. He looked wretched, but he deserved to be wretched, didn't he? 'You used every tactic in the book. And you didn't realise it?'

'I thought we were just scoring points.' He sighed. 'Hell, it was a game. I thought you knew that.'

'A game!' Tears stung her eyes as an incredulous laugh broke out of her.

'Until that last time,' he said softly. 'And then you know what happened. It took us both by surprise. Christiana, you've got to believe that I never meant to hurt you. I know you hate me, but at least believe me.'

Choking back the tears, she blinked hard, watching the garden. 'Well! So tell me about this very fortunate lady.'

The sarcasm in her voice made him frown. 'It's me you're mad at. Don't take it out on Dee.'

'I wouldn't dream of being that small-minded. Is that her name—Dee?'

He stood by her drawing board, all his smiles vanished now. 'It's short for Debra.'

'Really!' She forced a laugh. 'You do have a passion for shortening names, don't you? So what is she like, your Dee?'

He thought about that. 'It's hard to describe someone in a few words. I've known her for a long time.'

'How sweet! A boy and girl thing, was it? I can't imagine why you've kept her waiting so long.'

'There are reasons,' he said quietly and she wondered if she imagined the pain deep in his eyes.

'And when are we going to meet the mysterious lady?'

'Soon, I hope.'

All the time, while he stood there watching her unhappily, there seemed to be elastic bands around them, stretched to the limit and trying to draw them together. She wanted to close the gap and know again the comfort of his arms.

'You'll be pleased to see her, I expect,' she said. 'You must have missed her.'

'Yes, I have,' he said at last.

Christiana caught her breath, clenched her hands. 'Damn you, Jason! Do you have to be so honest?'

'You want me to lie to you?'

'Yes!' she cried.

'I can't break off the engagement,' he said in a low voice. 'There's no way I can do that to Dee.'

Her head felt about to explode with all the tears building up inside her while this dreadful interview went on. She wished he would leave, but she wanted him to stay. Her only defence was to draw back into a shell of lofty indifference.

Letting out a sharp laugh, she looked at him across her shoulder. 'I should hope not! Poor girl, I don't envy her the life she's going to have with you. Does she know you have this habit of seducing every woman who crosses your path?'

She could detect no expression on his face, as though he had shut off all his emotions. He walked slowly across to the door, making the floor echo to his steps. 'Good-bye, Christiana,' was all he said before he left.

* * *

'I never thought it would come to this,' her mother said sadly, standing in the bedroom doorway as Christiana gathered the last of her belongings. 'I know something happened between you and Jason, but surely you don't have to leave home because of it? It's not as though you have to see him all the time.'

'This has nothing to do with Jason,' Christiana replied for what seemed the hundredth time. 'We've been over all this before, Mother. I'm almost twenty-five. I need to be independent and manage on my own. With so many commissions coming my way, I really need to be in London. You ought to be grateful it's not Australia.'

'It's not your going I mind, it's the reasons for it.' Her mother sighed. 'Oh, Chris, if things don't work out, promise you'll come home.'

'I promise.' Christiana kissed her mother's cheek. 'Now I really must go. I'll call you this evening, OK?'

'OK.' Mrs Deverill wasn't happy, but nothing could dent her daughter's determination.

It really was time she untied the apron strings, Christiana assured herself as she headed south on the motorway. All Jason had done was provide the impetus for her to leave Arndale. She had made light of the whole thing to her parents, though she knew they remained concerned for her; they knew her too well not to comprehend her recent reticence and her newly-acquired habit of taking long walks.

A month's passing had not lessened the hurt. She had a feeling that this particular wound was going to fester for a long time.

She had been lucky to find a flat so soon after starting house-hunting. It was in a block on the edges of Kensington, not far from Hyde Park, and she had taken a year's lease on it.

As the summer passed, her longing for Jason subsided to a nagging emptiness that would catch her unawares at times and make her look at the phone, wanting to call him, but she never did. He was out of reach in the only way that mattered; he was engaged to his Dee, whom he missed, who would soon be coming to join him. Whatever he had felt for Christiana—and she knew he had felt something—it had not been strong enough to break the ties that bound him to the unknown Dee.

To stop herself from brooding, she flung herself into work and building a social life. She was drawn into the circle of a couple named Leon and Peg Reynolds. Leon owned a fabrics firm which used Christiana's designs; his wife, Peg, reminded Christiana of her own mother. They often asked her to dine with them and provided her with pleasant escorts, though their matchmaking didn't meet with much success.

Men seemed to find Christiana's cool friendliness enticing, though after a while she heard rumours that behind her back she was known as 'Miss Untouchable' and 'Miss Iceheart.'

In the darkness of night, however, with the continuous hum of London around her, she often found herself reliving those moments with Jason in the sunlit glade. The feelings between them had been mutual, she was sure of it. The memories haunted her, making her ache for the strength of his arms and the taste of his mouth until she turned her face into her pillow and wept . . .

* * *

At the end of August, Christiana took a holiday in Italy, driving a hired car round the historical sights or lazing on a sunlit beach.

On her return to London, she telephoned Arnside House and was horrified to discover that her mother had been rushed into hospital for tests.

'She hasn't been well all summer,' Christiana's father told her, his voice revealing his worry. 'I thought she was just missing you. But now . . . I just don't know, Chris. The doctors won't commit themselves until they've got the results of the tests. I know you've just been on holiday, but do you think you could come home, if only for a day or two?'

'I'll be there tomorrow,' Christiana said.

The countryside made her heart rejoice, next day. She had not realised how much she had missed the open spaces. The trees were just touched with gold and the fields were all striped with black where the stubble had been burned.

When she turned off the main road, every farm displayed signs advertising apples for picking, or fresh vegetables at cut prices. Almost home, Christiana stopped and bought a bunch of glorious flowers from a roadside stall.

Since her father would still be at the office, she drove straight to the hospital in Medfordham and was shown to a private room where her mother lay, pale and tired-looking. Several vases of flowers decked the room, and a display of get-well cards stood on the bedside cabinet.

Christiana paused in the doorway, seeing her mother's face light up at the sight of her. 'What's all this then?' she asked lightly. 'Felt like a rest, did you?'

'It's silly, isn't it?' her mother replied. 'Oh, Chris, it's good to see you, but you really shouldn't have come all this way. I know you're busy.'

'That's one good thing about freelancing,' Christiana replied. 'I can work when it suits me.' She bent to kiss her mother's cheek and laid the flowers on the bed.

'The roses came from Jason,' Mrs Deverill told her daughter.

Pain shot through Christiana, taking her breath away momentarily, but she covered it by glancing again at the roses, saying casually, 'How kind of him. So what's the news? Have you got the results of the tests yet?'

'Yes. This morning. It seems I've got kidney stones. Oh, I don't think it's anything to worry about,' she added swiftly as Christiana frowned. 'Usually they can dissolve the stones, but I have to stay in hospital for a while to make sure. The doctor explained it all in great detail. He's nice, you'd like him.'

'So long as he knows what's wrong,' Christiana replied, worried by the yellow tinge in her mother's skin. 'What's been happening in Arndale lately? Any juicy gossip?'

'Not that I know of. Apart from Beth Fleming having yet another boy friend—a friend of Brian's, apparently. They all go hang-gliding together, if you can believe it. But tell me about Italy. You're so brown! You look wonderful, Chris. I like your hair a bit shorter. And that suit's very elegant.'

'Thank you. It's the new me. Everything's going marvellously lately.'

Her mother's expression said she wasn't fooled. 'So you're happy?'

'Completely,' Christiana lied. 'When you're better, you must come to spend a few days with me, you and Dad. It would make a change for you.'

'That would be nice.' Mrs Deverill laid her hand over Christiana's as she added quietly, 'I think you did the right thing, Chris. I won't say I was happy about it, but that was just being selfish. You needed to get away, I know that. If it's all working out for you I'm glad.'

'It couldn't be better.'

Her mother's fingers squeezed in understanding. 'I suppose you know that Jason's fiancée's coming over here soon?'

An aching stillness descended on Christiana, but she managed to say, 'How would I have known that?'

'I just wondered,' Mrs Deverill said, troubled.

'How's he doing at Deverill's?' Christiana asked.

'Oh, settling in pretty well, I think. Your father has total faith in Jason. The two of them get along very well, though I don't see much of Jason myself. He bought a house, you know.'

'Where?'

'Out in the wilds somewhere. From what I've heard, it's not so much a house as a cottage. Modernised and everything, but you know what it's like up in Gravendale miles from anywhere, no neighbours, nothing. But Jason seems to spend all his free time up there.'

'Probably getting the place ready for when Dee comes,' Christiana said, as though the words didn't taste like ashes in her mouth. She felt the familiar agony of tears building up in her head, and kept them from her eyes only by an effort of will. 'Are they getting married over here?'

'I don't know. You know what your father's like—he'd never pry into anybody's private life unless they volunteered the information. Jason is his own man, I suppose.'

'Well, we'll find out soon enough,' Christiana replied. 'What matters is for you to get well again. I'll stay for a few days, to keep Dad company.'

She and her father talked mainly about her mother, neither of them openly admitting their worries that the cause of her illness might be more than kidney stones. But her doctor seemed confident enough, though the treatment would take time.

In the back of her mind, Christiana kept thinking about that cottage up in Gravendale, which she recalled as being a bleak valley, enclosed by sweeping fells where sheep grazed. Dry stone walls lay on the face of the land like a loose web of grey against tough grass and the silver trickle of streams which tumbled in small waterfalls. It seemed an unlikely place for Jason to be living.

In her spare time, she renewed her acquaintance with the dales, loving the feeling of space and mellow warmth that came with the end of summer. In London, everything was so crowded, and everyone was in such a hurry.

She told herself that it was sheer coincidence, allied with a certain amount of curiosity, which took her driving up towards Gravendale on a breezy day, when she assumed Jason would be safely at the office. She parked her car by a bridge at the end of the dale.

Climbing a gate, she walked up a hill, among grazing sheep that ambled aside as she passed.

From the summit, she could see down the length of Gravendale, where the road angled up between the hills to darker, heathery summits. Only one cottage stood in that expanse of land, a low building with grey stone walls, a brown stone-slate roof and small windows, tucked into the shelter of a cluster of yet more sycamores. A black car stood outside the cottage, though Christiana didn't register the significance of the vehicle's being there.

What had possessed him to come and live here, she wondered. It didn't fit his image of the go-ahead young business tycoon, but then, what did she really know about him?

Suddenly sensing another presence, she turned round and found Jason just three feet away, watching her with unreadable eyes. Taken completely off-guard, she gasped, 'Where did you spring from?'

'I was just about to ask you the same thing,'

he said with a slight smile that made his smoky-green eyes gleam in his tanned face. 'Is that a new car back by the bridge?'

'Oh, yes.' She glanced back at the trees clustering thickly along the stream below.

'Pretty racy car for a girl, isn't it?' he remarked.

Christiana looked back at him, having trouble with her comprehension. 'Sorry?'

'The car. It's pretty powerful.'

Oh, she should never have come, she thought in despair. She had forgotten how his presence disturbed her. He hadn't changed. I love you, she thought in agony. Jason, I love you.

'That's why I bought it,' she said eventually. 'I like sports cars. And I happen to be a good driver—"girl" or not.'

'I'm glad to hear it. Would it be wrong of me to ask just what you're doing here?'

'Oh, I was out for a drive and stopped for a breath of air. I miss the hills.'

Jason watched her levelly for a moment, seeing into her soul, or so it seemed. 'You mean, you didn't know this is where I live?'

'I—' About to deny it, she stopped herself. She had done it again, made a fool of herself, appeared to be chasing him when he had carefully been avoiding her. 'Yes, of course I knew,' she admitted quietly. 'But I thought you would be at the office. Mother told me you'd bought a place up here and I was curious.

Something wrong with that?'

'No, not that I can see.'

She half-turned away, gesturing down at the cottage. 'Is that it?'

'That's it.'

'It's not what I'd imagined. You like it?'

'It's OK,' he said. 'Plenty of fresh air. I get to walk, and do some climbing. Keeps me in shape.'

'Yes.' Despite herself, her glance ran over his athletic frame, which was obviously in excellent condition. She closed her eyes tightly and turned away from him, willing away the mounting desire to touch him, to be in his arms. 'I hear Dee is coming soon,' she blurted out.

'Saturday.'

'You'll be glad to see her.'

'Yes, I guess I will.'

She managed a shaky laugh. 'You only guess? Don't you know? Will . . .' the words nearly choked her, but she had to know. 'Will you be getting married soon?'

'We plan it for New Year's,' he said simply. 'In Milwaukee.'

'A winter wedding— how lovely. Will there be snow?'

'I guess . . .'

She thought of all kinds of bright, inane, lying remarks she might make, but she wasn't fooling him for a minute. He stared at her with such sorrow that she could have wept.

'I'm glad I didn't go into the office today. I miss you, Chrissy,' he said gruffly.

She winced as though he had driven a fist into her stomach. 'Don't say that! It's not me you miss, it's Dee.'

'It's you,' he said, shaking his head sadly.

'Jason . . .' His name was a croak caught on a sob as very slowly he reached for her. Her hands spread against his shirt where her palms came alive to the firm warmth of him as he drew her closer and closer.

'Don't,' she pleaded brokenly. 'Please . . .' But she was mesmerised by the sorrow in his eyes. Her mouth lifted and softened and she closed her eyes as he kissed her softly.

Despair shuddered through her. Her hands slid behind his neck and she felt herself being folded close to his body. She could not deny the relief of being close to him after so long a time of missing him. With an effort, however, she broke free, stumbling backwards with tears rolling down her face.

'You're not being fair, Jason!' She turned from him, running away down the hill.

She was halfway home before she could control her weeping, and then she wondered how she could have driven in such a state. It was a miracle she hadn't killed herself, and then what would her parents have done? They had enough problems. It occurred to her that death would have ended her personal agony, but she thrust the thought away as being immature and unrealistic. She was Christiana Deverill, was she not? She would find a way out of this unhappiness, somehow.

CHAPTER FOUR

That evening, Brian Fleming phoned Christiana to invite her to spend Saturday watching a hang-gliding competition at Whitestonecliff.

As it turned out, the day was fine, the company amusing, and the action fascinating. Beth, Brian's sister, was there with her latest boy friend, a young man with a wry sense of humour and infectious laugh. For minutes on end Christiana actually forgot all about Jason. The problem was not those minutes, but the hours when she could think of nothing else.

Dee was to arrive today . . .

'Pity it has to end,' Brian said as he brought his car to a halt on the gravel drive fronting Arnside House. 'The day I mean, I've really enjoyed it.'

'So have I,' Christiana replied.

'Then . . .' A sidelong glance from grey eyes awaited her reaction. 'How about having dinner with me?'

'Lovely!' Christiana said. Anything to stop her wondering what was going on in that lonely cottage . . .

While she prepared for her date with Brian, she pictured the scene with terrible clarity—a firelit room, a girl with masses of shining hair, long legs, bright eyes, and an enticing mouth that Jason would kiss as only he could kiss.

Christiana forced herself to imagine their wedding right to the bitter ending of snow and fairylights, when a beautiful bride would toss her bouquet to a pretty bridesmaid and turn to melt into the arms of her tender bridegroom and be carried away on a romantic honeymoon for two. Mr and Mrs Jason Straker . . .

She couldn't bear it, she thought, but she knew she was going to have to bear it. Jason had made it quite clear he had no intention of changing his plans.

Watching her come down the stairs, Brian whistled under his breath. 'You look great, Christiana. London's been good for you. It's given you . . .'

'Polish?' she suggested lightly. 'Thank you, Brian. You look very nice, too.' It was a pity she couldn't think of him as more than a friend . . .

He had booked a table at the best hotel in town, probably in the hope of impressing Christiana. It did impress her slightly, she had never thought Brian had that much imagination. The dining-room was decked with flowers, each table an island of candleglow.

'We're splitting the cost of this,' Christiana said. 'No, don't argue, Brian. I'm earning just as much as you are.'

'Is that what you do in London?' he demanded.

'It depends.'

'You wouldn't offer to pay half if you were with Jason Straker,' he accused. 'Don't insult me, Christiana. The first time I get you to come out with me and—'

'All right, Brian,' she conceded quietly. 'If you insist, thank you.'

As the meal progressed, she discovered that Brian found it hard to make conversation except about his various hobbies and, of course, his work. He couldn't seem to relate to her life in London, her career, or even her holiday in Italy.

'Good grief!' he said suddenly, his eyes fixed beyond her. 'Don't look now, but Jason Straker's over there with a girl. Is that his fiancée?'

Despite his admonishment not to look, she could not prevent a glance over her shoulder. At a table by the door, a dinner-jacketed Jason was smiling at something his companion was saying.

It had to be Dee, and she was just as stunning as Christiana had feared: blonde with a laughing red mouth, and eyes that could be seen to be devouring Jason alive in the candlelight that illumined their faces. As she waved her hands animatedly, light caught in the facets of a huge jewel in her engagement ring.

'Lucky so-and-so!' Brian muttered to himself. 'No wonder lie's been like a bear with a sore head lately. So would I be, a thousand miles away from . . .' He tore his eyes away from the couple across the room, glancing guiltily at Christiana. 'Sorry.'

'For what?' she asked with a shrug. 'You're right, she's stunning. What else did you expect?'

If it had been possible, she would have escaped without being seen by either Jason or his fiancée, but their table was as near the only exit and Brian insisted that they ought at least to say hello and welcome the newcomer to Britain. He led the way, dragging her behind him, and when Jason saw them coming he froze.

'Good evening, Mr Straker,' Brian greeted him.

'Brian,' Jason replied with a nod as he rose from his chair, his eyes turning to Christiana.

Using every ounce of her willpower, she managed to say casually, 'Hello, Jason.'

'We thought we'd just stop by and say hello,' Brian was saying, looking with open curiosity at Dee.

'This is Brian Fleming,' Jason informed his fiancée. 'And Miss Deverill. My fiancée, Dee Sloan.'

Looking delighted to meet them, Dee extended her hand first to Brian and then to Christiana. 'I thought it would be a while before I got to know any of you,' she said with pleasure. 'I want to thank you for taking such good care of Jason for me. Oh, excuse me not getting up.' A little smiling shrug and a gesture indicated her chair. 'This crazy seating arrangement of mine.'

It was, Christiana saw with a chill shock of horror, a wheelchair, of the latest design, neat and unobtrusive, but nevertheless a wheelchair.

'I broke my back,' Dee said. 'I'm not sick, I just have wheels instead of legs. I hope it won't make any difference.'

'Good heavens,' Brian said heavily. 'What difference could it make? To us, I mean. It must make a big difference to you, though. I'm very sorry, Miss . . .'

'Sloan,' Dee supplied in her sweet, girlish voice. 'But it's Dee to you. I'll call you Brian. You won't mind, will you? You work with Jason?'

While the two were occupied in talking to each other, Christiana slowly lifted her eyes to Jason's. Disabled, she thought. But how badly disabled? Jason, why didn't you tell me?

His eyes pleaded with her to be nice to Dee. Was he afraid she might upset Dee?

Unable to bear that unspoken, imaginary conversation, she glanced again at Dee's pretty face. The lovely features were framed in a tumble of curls whose ash-blonde paleness was a gift from nature. She was like a doll, small and perfect in every respect, but for that chair.

How long ago had the accident happened,

Christiana wondered, pity and frustration flowing through her.

'Well, we'll let you finish your meal,' Brian was saying, a possessive hand under Christiana's elbow. 'Good-night, Dee. Good-night, Mr Straker.'

Outside in the cool night air, he paused to glance at Christiana in the light from the hotel entrance. 'She can't be like that for ever, can she?' he said incredulously.

'If she broke her back . . .' Christiana muttered.

'Injured her spinal cord, I suppose. You'd think Straker would have told us, wouldn't you? I mean to say, suppose somebody goes and says something tactless? People ought to be warned beforehand, for her sake.'

So he had felt it, too, that immediate protective response toward the crippled Dee. She herself had experienced it, and how much stronger it must be in men, especially someone like Jason. It was odd, but she had expected to hate Dee, and now she found herself pitying her and even admiring her courage.

Suddenly, there was no contest. Christiana was defeated before she began.

They found Arnside House in darkness, Mr Deverill not having returned from a visit to the hospital.

'I expect he's gone over to see my aunt and uncle,' Christiana surmised. 'He said he might call there. Would you like to come in for a coffee, Brian?'

He accepted. She made coffee and they sat together on the settee, Brian going on and on about Dee until Christiana thought she might scream.

At length, he slid nearer, an arm along the settee behind her. 'I've really enjoyed tonight, you know,' he said, his glance roaming over her face. 'Can we do it again? How long will you be staying?'

'I'm going back tomorrow.'

'You never said,' he remarked, surprised.

'I only decided tonight.'

'I see.' A frown furrowed his brow, clearing as he looked at her mouth. 'Can I kiss you?'

'I thought you'd never get round to it,' she murmured, leaning her head on his arm. She wanted him to kiss her, to see if he could make her forget how very badly she was missing Jason Straker.

Brian ducked his head, tentatively touching his lips to hers for a brief moment. He looked as though he didn't believe his luck as he searched her eyes. She let her arm loop round his neck, responding with a curious detachment, as if she wasn't really involved.

Brian's arms came round her, his body pinning her against the settee as he leaned over her. She clung to him in desperation, willing him to make her forget Jason.

Suddenly, he became still. He drew away, frowning at her, his hand dragging her arm from round his neck. 'Why are you doing this?' he demanded, and wrenched himself to his feet. 'You've never let me near you before, and now, suddenly . . . It's because of Straker, isn't it? Because Jason Straker's fiancée has arrived? What are you trying to do, get back at him for what he did to you?'

Christiana sat up, straightening her jacket. 'I don't know what you mean, Brian.'

'And don't come the boss's daughter with me!' he exclaimed. 'Everybody knows the two of you had something going. And then there was a bust-up, wasn't there? That's why you went away. Everybody knows it.'

The news that she and Jason had been the subject of gossip brought Christiana to her feet. 'There's nothing to know!'

'Look . . .' He held out his hand in appeal. 'There's no reason for us to quarrel about this—I understand. But of course people know. This is a small community. Look at how you danced with him at the Mayor's Ball. And what about what happened at that charity auction at Easter? And at the cricket match? He came and joined you and your mother, then he followed you into the woods and neither of you came back. Then suddenly you go to London and we all find out he's engaged to be married. Of course people talked about it! You're Arthur Deverill's daughter, and he's the American takeover merchant. You weren't very discreet, Christiana.'

It was all true, of course, though at the time she hadn't realised how people would fit the pieces together and come up with such an accurate assessment of the situation. She flung her hands to her face as tears came streaming down.

When Brian took hold of her, she leaned on him and wept bitterly.

'Don't do that,' he pleaded. 'He's not worth it.'

'I know that!' she cried, jerking free of him. 'Do you think I don't know what a fool I've been? He's robbed me of everything—my home, my family, my pride. And now my reputation.'

'Then don't let him take your father's company, too.'

Through misty eyes, she gaped at him. 'What?'

His face was set, a touch of steel in the taut line of his jaw and the level grey eyes that watched her from two feet away. 'You heard what I said. And I know what I'm talking about. I see all the books, remember?'

This was a different Brian from the ill-at-ease man she had dined with. Now he was on solid ground, in his own world of finance and statistics.

'What are you telling me?' she asked incredulously.

'Just what I suspect. You remember we spoke once about the possibility of this being the beginnings of a takeover bid? Well, I think we got it wrong. It's not a takeover, it's a campaign for the destruction of Deverill's. We're in competition with Straker's in the States. Last year we won a big order which they'd been hoping for. We're getting in their way, so they've sent a man to put us out of business.'

'Brian . . .' she began helplessly. 'Oh, that can't be true! What evidence—'

'Not much, so far—Jason's been too clever. But the trouble's beginning. The workforce doesn't like his methods. He's even changed the way we do the accounts, which has caused a lot of ill-feeling and plenty of headaches for me. He's had time and motion study experts in to streamline jobs, which has meant a few redundancies on the shop floor, and that hasn't pleased the union. They've been talking about possible strike action—and that will mean losing orders, probably to Straker's.'

'Stop it, Brian!' she exclaimed. 'I can't believe any of this. I know he's made some changes, but my father trusts him. You know what they say about a new broom . . .'

'Have it your way. Just don't say I didn't try to warn you. I'd better go.' He stepped towards her, took her face between his hands and kissed her softly on the lips. 'Good-night, Christiana. Sleep well.'

* * *

Since her mother appeared to be recovering, if slowly, Christiana returned to London the following day. She had work to do, though she planned to take another few days off to come home when her mother eventually came out of hospital.

As the days passed, her thoughts dwelled on Yorkshire, where her mother was still in hospital, her father alone at Arnside House, where Jason and Dee were together at the cottage in the hills, and where odd things were happening at Deverill's.

She tried to tell herself that Jason would never do anything deliberately to harm the company, but her doubts grew.

She began to realise, though deep inside she had known for a long time, that she was not happy with city life. She had been born and raised in the country and though she enjoyed London for short periods, living there was too stressful to be comfortable. Her work could easily be done from home, with trips to London when necessary.

Before she made any final decision, she went home again to be on hand when her mother came out of hospital. She had only been gone from Yorkshire for about ten days, but already September was bringing flame to the trees.

She and her father paid a visit to the hospital that evening, making arrangements to collect her mother the following day. Then, as they drove back down the hill into the centre of town, Mr Deverill slowed the car.

'What is it?' Christiana asked.

'I'm not sure. Maybe I was seeing things. Do you mind if we go round by the factory while we're here? I could have sworn I saw a fire somewhere over there. No, you can't see it now, we're too far down the hill.'

Deverill's lay on the outskirts of Medfordham, its huge works buildings and office blocks sprawling beside a rough road which itself ran by the river Arn. As the car turned into the riverside lane, Christiana saw that her father's fears had been justified—there were flames leaping behind the windows of the upper floor of the office block behind big gates in a high wall.

'What the hell are the security men doing?' he raged aloud as he slammed on the brakes and leapt from the car.

The area was largely in darkness, a few lights shining across the expanse of the entrance and in farther corners, so that the red glare from the office block was startlingly clear.

Mr Deverill ran across to the gates, ringing the bell in the wall. After a moment or two, a security guard came ambling into sight, breaking into a run as he, too, saw the flames, and his boss.

'What's happened to the alarm system?' Mr

Deverill shouted. 'Phone 999, for God's sake!'

After a few seconds of confusion, he and the security man disappeared beyond the gate and Christiana climbed out of the car. As she crossed the road, a window in the office block shattered and flame spilled out—the fire was spreading fast. How on earth could it have started so long after work finished for the night? Unless someone had deliberately lit it!

She ran towards the gate, becoming aware of someone else emerging from the deep shadows thrown by the wall. As she glanced at him he grabbed her, saying, 'Stay away from there, Chris!'

'Jason!' A second ago she had been thinking about arson; now all at once she was remembering what Brian had said about a campaign of destruction. Was this another step along that road? Where had Jason come from at this hour of the night? She was unsteady on her feet, her hands grasping his arms as she stared up at him, saying in a strangled voice, 'What are you doing here?'

The question made his glance flick over her face as his mouth tightened. 'What do you think I'm doing? Get out of my way! And don't come any farther.'

Then he was gone, sprinting through the gate to where the glow of security lights could be seen in the lobby of the administration building.

He had a key. Of course he had a key.

Within seconds he had disappeared inside the building. On the upper floor the red glow had spread to three more windows. Christiana stood watching, holding her breath, terrified for him.

'Was that Jason?' her father demanded, returning at a run to join her. 'What's the idiot up to? It's beyond our control! What's happened to the alarm, and the sprinkler system?'

They've been turned off, she thought. Someone meant to burn the place down. Someone . . . She glanced along the wall, where in the deep shadows now she could make out the shape of a car—Jason's car. Had it been there when she and her father drove past? She couldn't remember. They had been too busy staring at the fire. But if the car had been there, then where had Jason been?

CHAPTER FIVE

In the distance, Christiana could hear the rise and fall of the fire engine's siren as it came hurtling through the town.

'We'd better get out of the way,' her father said, calling to the hovering security men. 'Here, open these gates. Chris, you move my car out of the way—well out of the way.'

By the time she had taken the car farther down the lane, the fire engines were coming at speed, sirens blaring, blue lights flashing, to screech in through the gates. Men leapt out, shouting instructions to each other as they unrolled hoses and prepared to attack the blaze.

Christiana found herself behind one of the gates. Water flew up into the sky, sending clouds of steam to join the rising smoke. She could see the lobby past the bulk of one of the engines, and to her relief she saw a figure come stumbling out. The chief fireman ran towards him, obviously telling him to get out of the way. Jason obeyed, fits of coughing bending him double as he made his way back to the gates. With concern, Christiana saw that he was clutching his right arm, and he was dripping wet.

'What were you trying to do, man?' Mr Deverill demanded. 'Are you hurt?'

'No, I'm OK,' Jason gasped.

'You're far from OK,' Mr Deverill said sternly. 'Where's your car? Let Chris have the keys. She'll take you up to the hospital.'

'I'm OK, I tell you!' Jason protested hoarsely. 'It's just the smoke—and I've done something to my arm. It's not broken or anything. There's no need for a hospital.'

'Well, you're certainly not driving in this state. Chris, take him back to Arnside House and look after him. I'd better stay here. Look, Jason, don't argue! I've too many other things on my mind. The most helpful thing you can do—both of you—is to get out of the way.'

He strode away to watch the firemen at work, and Christiana saw that Jason's face was streaked with black and water trickled from his flattened hair. He still clutched his arm, though when she asked about it, he shouted at her, 'I said it's not broken! It's just bruised.'

'Sorry I asked!' she snapped. 'So where are your car keys?'

'In my pants' pocket—the right side.'

'Let's go. And don't glare at me, Jason! Just let's get you home. Then I'll take a look at your arm.'

To her relief he didn't argue further, though she sensed the bleakness of his mood all the way back to Arnside House.

She showed him the bathroom, provided fresh towels and a dressing-gown belonging to her father, and then she left him to take a shower.

'I'll be downstairs. Shout if you need me.'

He gave her a glowering look. 'I'll do that.'

'Are you sure you can manage?'

'Get lost!' he roared at her.

Christiana stiffened, offended and hurt. 'I was only trying—'

'I know what you were trying to do. Don't fuss. Get out of here, will you?'

Going down to the sitting-room, she poured herself a drink and sat worrying, unable to prevent herself from thinking about Jason's possible involvement in the fire. What had he been doing in Medfordham well after nine at night? Why had he rushed into the burning building?

'What do I do about my clothes?' he asked, appearing in the doorway, wearing her father's dressing-gown, which left his legs bare to above the knee. His face was set in grim lines and his hair was still wet, dishevelled by towelling.

'Where are they?' she asked.

'In the bathroom.'

'Then I'll deal with them. You pour yourself a drink. And there's a comb in my bag—over there—if you need it.'

As she passed him, he caught her arm, making her stop and lift questioning eyes to his face. 'I'm sorry I yelled at you,' he said.

'That's all right,' she replied, her voice husky as she remembered how frightened she had been of losing him in that fire. Now he stood beside her, looking vulnerable in that ridiculous dressing-gown with his hair all on end like a little boy and his eyes heavy with regret. 'How's your arm?' she asked.

He glanced down at it. 'Like I said—bruised. I fell across the stairs. Look.' He brushed back the sleeve of the dressing-gown, showing her a muscular forearm covered in curling dark hairs, and with a blue weal across the muscle. 'Lucky I'm pretty tough,' he commented.

Clenching her hands so that they couldn't touch him to soothe his hurt, she said worriedly, 'Are you sure it's not broken? We ought to have gone to the hospital, you know.'

'There's no need. I've had enough broken bones in my time to know the difference. I used to play football—our type of football—at college.'

'Oh?' She glanced up at his face again, saddened. How little she knew about him. 'Well, I'll go and stick your clothes in the washing machine. Make yourself at home.'

'Sure,' he said, and as she went up the stairs, she wondered why he sounded so mournful.

Fortunately all his clothes could go in on the same fabric programme. She switched the washing machine on and left it to do its work while she returned to the sitting-room where Jason sat brooding over a glass of whisky.

'Would you like me to call Dee?' she asked.

'No!' he said swiftly. 'No, don't worry her.'

'Worry her?' she queried. 'Won't she be worried anyway, wondering where you are?'

'She'll think I'm at home,' Jason said, much to her bewilderment. His expression hardened as he read her mind and added, 'You think that's where she is—at the cottage?'

'Well . . . isn't she?'

He watched her from under his brows, his face unreadable. 'She's living at the Grand Hotel in Medfordham.'

'Since when?'

'Since she arrived over here.'

'Can she look after herself ?' she asked.

'For some things. But she has a private nurse with her. That's where I'd been this evening—to see her. She's coming down with a cold, so I left early. I saw the fire from across town.'

So that was the explanation! Relieved, she sat down opposite him in an armchair. 'So did we. We were coming from the hospital.'

'Oh, I see.' He looked down into his glass, swirled the whisky round and drained it in one gulp.

'Would you like some more?' Christiana asked, leaving her seat to take his glass and moving across the room to the drinks cupboard.

She didn't hear him move, but as she poured whisky he said quietly from immediately behind her, 'I thought you were in

London.'

'I came back today,' she managed to say. 'To be home when Mother gets out of hospital tomorrow.'

'She'll be glad you're here,' he murmured, the deep, caressing timbre of his voice sending shivers up and down her spine.

She felt him touch her hair, very lightly, and she jerked round, almost spilling the whisky. 'Don't!'

His eyes flickered, surveying every inch of her face with undisguised hunger, then with a sad smile, he took the glass from her. 'OK, Chrissy. If you say so.'

Knowing that if she stayed where she was for another second they would both give in to the magnetic force that seemed to be drawing them together, Christiana walked swiftly away, saying, 'I wonder if they've contained the fire yet? I wish Dad would phone. I'd better go and make the bed in the spare room. You'll have to stay here tonight.'

'I guess I shall,' Jason said softly, and gave her another wry smile.

She made the spare bed with unnecessary care, taking as much time as was possible. Being alone with Jason was dangerous. She was well aware that one unguarded move would take them into a situation which could only lead to more pain and trouble for all concerned. He wanted her, that was clear, but she couldn't fool herself into thinking that he loved her, too.

Oh, yes, she wanted him, shamefully, with or without his love, but she knew that if it began it would never be enough for her. She wanted him completely, for always. For both their sakes it was best to fight off temptation.

When she returned to the sitting-room, Jason seemed to have reached much the same conclusion. They sat apart, talking of anything trivial. Occasionally, the conversation faltered and anguish intervened, silent and unmentioned, but known to both of them. It was probably the hardest two hours of Christiana's life so far, until at last she heard a car draw up outside and her father came in, weary and depressed.

'It's a mess.' He sighed. 'I suppose it could have been worse, but even so it's bad enough. The police think it was arson. Would you believe they found some petrol cans left behind? As blatant as that!'

Christiana didn't look at Jason; she was too afraid he might see the terrible suspicions that were in her mind before she could stop them. But she dismissed them at once.

'Come and have a drink, Dad,' she suggested. 'Nothing will look so bad in the morning.'

* * *

Mrs Deverill had lost a good deal of weight

and in moving back to Arnside House it became clear that she would not be fully fit for some time. Of course, they had Mrs Jeavons, who came in every weekday to help with the housework, but normally Mrs Deverill did her share of the chores and cooking. Christiana knew she was going to be needed at home.

On her way back from a shopping trip to Medfordham, she called in at Deverill's to see for herself what was happening. Most of the staff, to their credit, were 'mucking in together' in order to get their work done, but there were one or two sour faces. Christiana found Brian Fleming in his shirt sleeves, trying to sort out a mass of papers damaged by water, in an office where chaos reigned.

'Your father's out somewhere,' he informed her. 'But I think Mr Straker's around if you want him.'

'I only came to take a look for myself,' she replied. 'Lord, what a mess! I won't stay. I can see you're busy.'

Brian grabbed his jacket from the back of a chair. 'I'll walk you to your car,' he said, adding to his colleagues, 'I won't be long.'

He wanted to speak to her, she thought. She hoped he didn't have bad news.

As they walked slowly across to the car park, Brian said, 'This is a hell of a business. You know it was arson, of course.'

'So Dad told me. Pretty clumsy, too, from what I gather.'

'Whoever it was must have been pretty sure he wouldn't be caught. There's no one specific person who might have done it. At least, not that the police know of.'

From the corner of her eye, Christiana gave him a troubled glance. 'I know what you're implying, Brian, and I still refuse to believe it. I was here—I saw Jason go in there, risking his life.'

'I heard,' Brian said flatly. 'Highly commendable of him. And it did tend to throw suspicion away from him, didn't it? All I can say is, it's lucky your father saw the fire. The security men were watching football on their portable TV, apparently, and someone had tampered with the alarm system. If the whole office block had gone up in smoke then we would have been in big trouble. A modern company revolves round its paperwork. Even as things stand there are bound to be some delays. But it could have been a lot worse if your father hadn't had his wits about him.'

'Jason saw the fire, too,' Christiana objected. 'That's why he was there. He was on his way back from seeing Dee.'

'So he says,' Brian qualified, pausing with her beside her car. 'Anyway, I'm glad you're here. How long are you staying?'

'A few more days. But I've been thinking . . . I'm not that happy in London, and I'm needed at home. I've made up my mind to come back to live. I can still do my work up here, the way

I always used to. Maybe I'll miss out on a few commissions, but it will be worth it for peace of mind.'

Clear grey eyes met hers levelly. 'And Straker?'

'He has nothing to do with it,' she assured him. 'All that is over. He and Dee are getting married just after Christmas.'

'Yes, so I heard. They seem very happy.'

'They ought to be,' she said. 'They're in love with each other. Look, Brian, I must go. Mother's expecting me home for lunch. I'll see you around.'

'You will,' he confirmed, laying a hand on her arm, his face serious as he looked her in the eye. 'Remember I'm here. If ever you need me, just yell and I'll come running. We're friends, Chris.' He leaned to kiss her briefly on the corner of her mouth, smiled at her and added, ' 'Bye for now.'

* * *

Having made arrangements for extra help in the house, Christiana returned to her flat in London and began to make plans for leaving. Her lease had eight months to run, but fortunately a young couple she knew were anxious for somewhere to live while they looked around for a permanent home, and they jumped at the chance of renting her furnished flat in the meantime.

Alone on her last night in London, Christiana lay awake listening to the hum of the city and wondering if she was doing the right thing. Returning to Yorkshire meant being near Jason, and though she had told Brian it was all over, she knew it to be a lie. She would never stop wanting Jason, if she lived to be a hundred.

So she came home.

The year had turned to October and as she drew up outside Arnside House, a cold wind blew rain along the dale.

'We've invited Jason and his fiancée to tea on Sunday,' her mother informed her almost as soon as she walked in the door. 'If you want to be somewhere else . . .'

'Why should I?' Christiana asked. 'I'd like the chance to meet Dee properly.'

Even so, she half-expected Jason to cancel the engagement when he discovered she had come home, but he did not. She told herself he was right; the madness between them was over, and if embers lingered they must be stamped out under a show of social politeness. If they avoided each other too obviously, people might start to talk, and Dee could hear rumours.

Christiana wore a lacy pink wool suit, with her hair pinned up in an elegant style. Looking at her reflection, she tried a bright smile and knew that when Dee arrived she must try even harder to keep that lost look out of her eyes.

From an upstairs window she watched as the car arrived, and Jason climbed out to take the invalid chair from the boot. He opened the passenger door and lifted Dee out, his head bent as she fastened her arms round his neck and laughed up at him. She was wearing a bright red coat against which her hair looked pale and silky, and as Jason placed her in the chair she kissed his cheek.

A laughing exchange took place between them, presumably because she had branded him with her lipstick, for Christiana saw him take a handkerchief from his suit pocket and scrub at his cheek, clearly asking Dee if the mark had gone.

They looked so comfortable together, so engrossed in each other, that Christiana had to fight back tears of bitter jealousy. She hurried back to her bedroom, where she forced deep breaths into her aching lungs and took a few minutes to rearrange her aura of cool sophistication.

They were all in the sitting-room when she went down. Dee wore a scarlet dress which matched the coat she had taken off, and her shapely legs were sleek in sheer tights, with high-heeled red shoes. She remained in her chair, smiling across the room as Mr Deverill made introductions.

'Oh, but we met.' Dee laughed. 'At the hotel that night, didn't we, Chris? I have to admit I was a bit jet-lagged, but I do remember that.

How's Brian?'

'Pretty well, as far as I know,' Christiana replied.

'I thought he was sweet,' Dee said. 'And you're a designer. How fascinating! Didn't you say it was fabrics, honey?' This was addressed to Jason, who had stood up on Christiana's arrival and was politely waiting for her to sit down.

Briefly, their eyes met, conveying their mutual discomfort, and Christiana sank into a chair, allowing him to resume his seat beside Dee.

As always happened when Christiana's career came up for discussion in that room, her father pointed out the portraits flanking the fireplace. Dee admired them with flattering warmth.

'It must be wonderful to have a talent like that,' she remarked in her clear, girlish voice. 'I'm not clever at anything.'

'Of course you are,' Jason contradicted. 'You play guitar. You write songs.'

Dee made a little face at him and smiled, reaching for his hand. 'Not with much success. But thanks for the confidence, honey.' She turned her smile on the three Deverills, adding. 'He's so good for me, I don't know what I'd do without him. To tell the truth I've been scared he might meet some fabulous English girl and fall in love with her.' Her melting blue eyes turned adoringly to

Jason's face.

Perhaps Christiana imagined the momentary awkward pause, but a second later her mother was asking how Dee liked England and Dee declared that she adored Yorkshire and couldn't wait to start married life there.

Behind her social smile, Christiana was miserable, forced to observe the closeness between Jason and his fiancee.

Just once during that time her glance connected with Jason's. She smiled, and he smiled, but before their eyes parted she saw the haunted shadows moving in smoky-green depths. Both of them were enduring their private hells.

It was a relief to her when the doorbell rang and she could jump up to answer it and escape from a room which, despite its size, was becoming claustrophobic.

'Mr Deverill?' inquired the tall, moustached man who stood on the doorstep. 'Would you tell him it's Detective Chief Inspector Ford, please?'

It transpired that he had come with information about the fire at the factory. Her father took him into the study, along with Jason, leaving the three women alone.

'That gives me a chance to get the tea ready,' Mrs Deverill said. 'No, it's all right, Chris, I can manage. You stay and talk to Dee. We've got nearly everything ready in the kitchen.'

'Your mother's sweet,' Dee commented as Mrs Deverill left the room. 'So's your father. I'm not sure what I expected, but everyone's been real nice to me. I just know I'm going to love it over here. I hope we'll be friends, Chris.'

'So do I,' Christiana said, praying that there would come a time when she could stop regarding Dee as a rival. Surely this hurt wouldn't go on for ever?

When Dee expressed a wish to see the garden, Christiana took her out by a side door, negotiating the chair carefully over a step and along winding pathways through a pergola to where a vista of the dale opened out.

The day was still and with the sun shining, the air remained warm, though the colours in the trees were fading and drifts of brown leaves gathered underfoot.

A contented sigh breathed out of Dee as she sat studying the view. 'I just love the fall, don't you?'

'Oh—yes,' Christiana lied, hardly able to say that she had always hated autumn; to her it presaged the coming of the dark winter days and the long months before spring returned. This year, especially, the approaching winter held even more bitterness—by the time spring came again, Dee would be Jason's wife.

'And I love your house,' Ike added.

A movement behind her made Christiana glance round to see Jason approaching, carrying a car blanket. He gave her the ghost of a smile and his eyes seemed to mirror the heavy sadness she was feeling. How fine he was, she thought, tall and strong, athletic and active. And how hard it was not to be able to share what was in her heart, not to be able to touch him or even look at him without fear of being observed.

Tears caught her unawares and she swung away, blinking hard to control the treacherous evidence of her feelings. Beside her, Jason bent to tuck the blanket round Dee's legs, saying, 'You'll get cold out here without your coat.'

'I'm just fine,' she replied softly, stroking his arm. 'But thank you, honey. You're sweet to worry about me so. I know I'm a nuisance.'

'You're not,' he said, and leaned to kiss her cheek.

Watching them, Christiana wanted to scream or run away. She had to clench her hands, take a deep breath, and pretend there was nothing wrong.

'I was just telling Chris how much I love her home,' Dee said as Jason straightened. 'Don't you think it's lovely, too, honey? The problem is, Chris, that any house we buy will have to be altered for me. Ramps and things. Hoist bars. I was never very tall, but in this silly chair I have trouble reaching everything. I don't know how Jason can stand it.'

'I've told you I don't mind,' he said, a hoarse

edge in his voice.

Dee took his hand, her lovely face lifted to look at him. 'And I love you for it, honey.' Her smile invited Christiana to join in her admiration. 'Don't you think I'm the luckiest girl in the world to have Jason? He's been so patient.' Memories clouded her blue eyes as she went on sadly, 'I was a model, did you know? Until the accident. I was on an assignment in Aspen, Colorado. A few of us went skiing. Next thing I know, I'm on my back in hospital and they tell me I'll never walk again. We had to postpone the wedding. I told Jason he could have his freedom, but—'

'Christiana's not interested in all that,' Jason interrupted brusquely. 'I think we ought to get you back inside. The wind's turning cold.'

There wasn't any wind, not that Christiana could feel, but she made no demur as Jason turned the chair with Dee in it and the three of them walked back beneath the pergola, where the prickly branches of a climbing rose were nearly bare of leaves.

'Will you do me a favour, Chris?' Dee asked.

'Of course. Just name it.'

'Will you do a portrait for me?'

'Why, yes, I'd love to.'

Dee glanced round, her face alight with smiles. 'You would? Oh, that's sweet of you. When we do get our house, I'd just adore to have a portrait of Jason where I can look at it all the time.'

'I can't afford the time,' Jason said, dismissing the idea. 'Have you any idea how long sittings take?'

Dee twisted in her chair to look at him, pouting. 'Oh, honey! You could use a few hours of your spare time, couldn't you? For me? Please?'

'I'll think about it,' he said. 'You've neither of you asked what the policeman wanted, and that's what's on my mind right now. He reckons they've got a lead on the arsonist. Maybe they'll track the guy down now.'

'Thank goodness for that,' Christiana said with a sigh of relief.

CHAPTER SIX

Christiana heard no more about the suggested portrait until ten days later when Jason phoned her late at night to say that Dee was still very keen on the idea. If it was convenient for Christiana, he could come over for a couple of hours that Saturday afternoon.

'That's fine,' she replied brightly, not voicing her disquiet. 'Yes, come around two o'clock. I'll have everything ready.'

In the meantime, when she had a spare few minutes, she sketched out the background she intended to use—an asymmetrical swirl in the autumn colours which Dee had said she loved. It would complement Jason's colouring to perfection.

By two o'clock on Saturday she had her easel set up, with a comfortable chair on a dais by the big window waiting for Jason. He arrived, wearing a sage-green sweater and slacks which she thought would be just right for her interpretation, but his mood was less obliging. He seemed edgy, despite her efforts to be impersonal and pretend he was just another sitter.

Her brush outlined his shape on the canvas, swiftly sketching in the main lines of his head and upper body. But every time she glanced up she met his sombre eyes, and when she looked away she was aware of his watching her, studying her with obvious misery. After a while, that awareness between them became too much to bear.

Jason stood up and massaged his shoulder irritably. 'I'm stiff. And I'm bored. I'm not used to sitting around doing nothing.'

'Well, how else can I paint you?' Christiana snapped, her nerves in shreds. 'What did you think you'd have to do? Oh—all right, we'll take a break. I'll make some coffee, shall I?'

He made no reply, remaining by the window, running his fingers again and again through his hair.

'Jason,' she tried again, 'would you like some coffee?'

That made him swing round, looking at her as though he hated her. 'What I want,' he growled, 'is to get out of here. Some other time, Chris.'

Helpless, she watched as he strode from the room.

He phoned from the office during the week, to apologise and suggest they might try again the following Saturday.

By the fourth Saturday sitting, the portrait was finished but for the final details. On the canvas, Jason looked like a rampaging tiger, poised for the kill. Unfortunately, she had managed to capture his exact expression as he watched her with tormented eyes. Just to look at the portrait made her stomach twist itself into knots of breathless tension. Dee would probably hate the picture, for it showed a side of Jason which was not normally on display.

As he sat again in her studio that final Saturday, Christiana remembered how he had been when she first met him—smiling, charming, teasing. Now he looked as if he might never smile again.

'How's it coming along?' he asked suddenly.

'Almost done.' She stepped back to look at the picture she had created, and she knew she didn't want to part with it. It held memories of all the bitter-sweeet hours they had spent in the studio together, together but separate, neither of them daring to admit to feelings which both knew were flaring between them.

'Can I look?' he asked. He came slowly, tense as a coiled spring as she backed away and left ample room for him to view the portrait. His eyebrows lifted in surprise. 'Is that how I look?'

'Well, you refused to smile. That's more or less how you look when you're serious. I'm not really a portrait painter, after all. Do I gather you don't like it?'

'I'm not sure I like what it says about me. I never knew I was that threatening. Is that the way I strike you—as dangerous?'

'No, not really. It's just the way you've been looking while you sat there. I didn't mean to catch it quite so accurately. You don't think anyone will read anything into it, do you?'

'Only us.' Without looking at her, he held out a hand towards her. After a brief hesitation she stretched out her own hand and felt his fingers twine with hers, hurtingly tight. The touch made her heart twist with pain. It was not nearly enough and yet it was too much.

'What are we going to do, Chris?' he asked in an undertone, still looking at the picture.

'Nothing,' she said hoarsely. 'There's nothing we can do, is there?'

'Seems not.' Shaking his head, he turned to show her the hopeless longing in his eyes. 'She needs me. She trusts me. I can't let her down.'

'I know,' she whispered. 'And I love you for it. Isn't that crazy? I love you all the more because you're going to . . .'

'Chrissy!' He pulled her nearer, his arms locking round her as his mouth found hers in a desperate kiss that made her senses reel. She clung to him, answering the wild seeking of his mouth with equal passion and despair.

'I love you,' he muttered, pressing his lips across her face. 'I love you, want you, need you. I can't bear being without you!'

A few days later, Christiana took the completed portrait to the hotel, after calling to make sure that Dee would be in. She was met at the door of the suite by a middle-aged woman whom she assumed to be the nurse.

Though it was mid-afternoon, Dee was wearing a lacy negligee as she lay propped up on a settee with a guitar beside her. She was perfectly groomed and made-up.

Christiana unwrapped the brown paper she had fastened round the portrait and held it for Dee to look at; so she saw the immediate dislike which Dee took to the picture.

'It's not what I expected,' she said slowly, then her smile reappeared. 'But I don't know the first thing about art. I guess I've no call to argue with you. You know best.'

'You hate it,' Christiana said with a sigh. 'I had a feeling you would. It's not very good, is it? Still, I thought I'd show it to you. I believe I warned you that portraits aren't really my forte.'

'Oh, it's fine!' Dee said. 'Just fine. It's just not Jason. Not my Jason. Couldn't you have made him smile, or something? Having him scowl like that frightens me. I guess I'd prefer a photograph—the way he really looks. But he'll pay you for your work, of course.'

'That won't be necessary.' Hastily, Christiana wrapped the portrait again, actually relieved that Dee didn't want it. It was a personal thing, between her and Jason, and she wanted it for herself. 'Jason wasn't very keen on it, either. But I can always paint over it. If nothing else, it's taught me to stick to what I do best in future.'

She escaped as soon as was polite, returning to Arnside House to hang the portrait in her studio, where it would be a constant reminder of the truth if ever she allowed herself to dream too wildly. However, the portrait was almost as bad as having Jason himself there; all it did was remind her that she could never have him. After a day or two of working under that tiger's glare, she took the portrait down and hid it away.

For consolation there was work, and a trip to London to discuss a new venture in co-ordinating fabrics, wallpaper and stencil designs which could be applied to plain-painted furniture. And there was always faithful, reliable, dear, dull Brian, with whom she played badminton on a fairly regular basis. One evening after badminton, instead of going on to a pub for a drink, she and Briam had coffee in the cafeteria at the sports centre, where they could look down on the blue expanse of the swimming pool through big glass windows.

Now that winter had arrived, the pool was less crowded and only a few energetic souls splashed in the shallows, while a couple of more serious swimmers ploughed up and down the lengths.

'I suppose you heard about the accident,' Brian said, watching his coffee swirl as he stirred in sugar.

'Accident?' Christiana queried. 'At Deverill's, you mean? No, what happened?'

Brian glanced up at her. 'It wasn't exactly an accident. Nothing actually happened, though it was a close call. Your father nearly got his brains bashed in at the works. They were moving some heavy machinery and somebody touched the wrong lever or something. At least, that's what everybody says.'

'Well, what else could have caused it?'

'It just seems funny to me that it happened just at that moment when your father was there. He isn't in the works that often. He didn't mention it, then?'

'Not in my hearing, and if he'd told Mother she would have repeated it to me. Brian, what exactly are you saying? That someone attempted murder?'

'No, not exactly,' he said, frowning. 'But it could have been a warning. We're in the middle of negotiating for a big order that will keep us in full production for two years. With things as they are in industry, you must know how important it is to keep the order book full. But it's the sort of deal that Straker's are bound to be putting in estimates for, too. So once again we're in competition with them. If anything happened to your father at this stage—'

'Brian, stop it!' she cried. 'You're getting paranoid over all this.'

'Am I? Well, I assure you it's not without cause. First the little niggles, then the fire, then a near-accident to your father, and next, probably, an all-out strike.'

'But my father says Jason's new ideas are

beginning to work for the good of the company.'

'I'm only telling you what I know,' Brian replied with a shrug. 'What you read into it is up to you. But something's eating Straker. See for yourself.'

He slanted a glance down at the pool, mystifying Christiana until she realised with a shock that one of the swimmers doing length after length was Jason. He swam strongly, under water for most of the way, doing a smooth and powerful breast stroke, then broke surface for a turn and came back slicing through the water in a crawl that ate up the distance in seconds. Back and forth, breast stroke and crawl, as if he were trying to wear himself out.

'That's what I wanted you to see,' Brian said. 'He's here nearly every night, for at least an hour, swimming up and down with hardly a break. Now, if I had Dee Sloan dangling on a string, I certainly wouldn't waste an hour every evening in a swimming pool, not unless I had something on my mind.'

'I'm going home to find out from my father what he thinks about this business at Deverill's. I don't believe you're right, Brian, but my father ought to know what's being said.'

*   *   *

Arthur Deverill, however, dismissed her fears with a laugh before she had time to do more than broach the subject. 'Good heavens, Chris, you haven't joined the anti-Straker league, have you? I know you've had your upsets with him, but . . .'

But Christiana couldn't forget about it. The more she tried to put it aside, the more questions built in her mind, until she knew she must do something about it.

What she did, eventually, was phone Jason at his cottage late one evening.

'Hello,' his voice said crisply.

'Jason?' was all she said, but it must have been enough for he replied at once, sounding as though he didn't believe his ears.

'Chris, is that you?'

'Yes. It's me. Hello.'

After a long pause, he said softly, 'Hello.'

Just hearing his voice made her shiver, but obviously he was waiting for her to explain herself. 'Jason, I . . . I need to talk to you.'

'Go ahead,' he invited.

'No, not over the phone.' Oh, Lord, she hadn't realised how difficult this was going to be. 'I have to see you. I know how this must sound but I can assure you I'm not chasing you. There's something I have to talk to you about. It's important.'

'You want to come over here some time? To the cottage?'

'No, not the cottage.'

'Then where?'

'I thought somewhere public.'

'Public?' he echoed incredulously. 'Why don't we just take out an advertisement in the local paper and have everyone turn up to view the proceedings? Are you crazy?'

'There's no need to be sarcastic,' she said stiffly. 'You know very well what I mean. Somewhere away from Medfordham. How about—do you know Welmond?'

'Sure.'

'Well, will you meet me there on Saturday? Say about three o'clock, by the market cross on the square.'

'You sound upset,' Jason said. 'What's wrong, sweetheart?'

She squeezed her eyes tight shut, whispering in anguish, 'Don't call me that! Just say you'll be there.'

'I'll be there,' he replied at once.

'Thank you,' she managed to say, and put the phone down, distressed almost beyond bearing.

CHAPTER SEVEN

Christiana was late for the appointment, held up by a huge lorry on one of the narrow byroads, but eventually she made it to Welmond and found a place to park just off the market square.

It was a bitter day in December, a wind driving odd flurries of thin snow across the market stalls. Despite a chill wind, a happy, expectant atmosphere prevailed among the crowds.

Pulling her woollen hat more closely round her head, Christiana threw the end of her scarf around her throat and began to wind her way between groups of people wandering around the market. Welmond was a small town and there was little reason for anyone from Medfordham to come. She saw no familiar faces among the throng.

The market cross stood in the centre of the cobbled square, a tall stone memorial to men killed in the wars. Beside it a lorry was parked, with a pile of crates higgledy-piggledy beside it and squashed cabbage leaves strewing the cobbles. It was hardly the ideal spot for a romantic rendezvous.

Then she saw Jason standing on the steps of the cross blowing on his hands and rubbing them to keep warm. His familiar figure was dressed in a thick green jacket with many zipped pockets on the sleeves and front. She saw him glance at his watch, stuff his hands in his pockets and shiver as he stamped his feet. A wave of tenderness caught her, making her pause behind the canvas protecting a sweet stall.

She took a few more steps before he caught sight of her. He looked cold, but his face lit in a half-smile as she hurried up to him, saying, 'I'm sorry I'm late. Have you been waiting long?'

'Half an hour,' he said ruefully. 'I came early. But it's good to see you, Chris. How are you?'

'I'm fine, thank you. You?'

'Can't complain.'

Their eyes met in a long glance fraught with unspoken communication, then he took her arm. 'Let's walk. There's a café over there. I could use a cup of coffee.'

The café was small, crowded, with steamy windows and indifferent coffee. They had to share a table with other people, so talking was impossible, except about the weather and Christmas. But beneath the table his hand found hers and held it tightly, while his eyes said things she had been longing to know. He had missed her, too.

Eventually they went out again to stroll round the market and seek the quieter streets which led down to the river. Behind them, the sound of carols grew fainter as they left the market.

'Dee's going home in a few days,' Jason said.

'Oh?'

'She's already stayed longer than she planned. She'll have a lot to do.'

'Of course.' She was grateful for his tact in not actually mentioning the wedding, though they both knew that was what would be occupying Dee. 'What about you? When will you be going?'

'I plan to be home for Christmas,' he replied.

They were walking slowly, side by side, not touching or looking at each other. Christiana huddled into her coat, hands in her pockets, her gaze on the wet pavement where light gleamed from windows of small shops.

Quietly, she said, 'I hope you'll be very happy.' And when he stopped walking she turned to look at him, her face feeling frozen from the wind. 'I mean it, Jason. I do hope you'll be happy. If you're not, then what's the point of it all?'

'Sometimes I wonder,' he muttered.

She resumed her slow pace, walking with dogged determination.

'You're cold,' he murmured, and as though it were the most natural thing in the world, he drew her into his arms to lean on him, his head bent over hers.

The sound of hurried footsteps approached down the street. Christiana tried to break free but he held her too firmly, murmuring in her ear, 'Stay where you are. Nobody knows us here. We're not doing anything wrong.'

The footsteps came past, heading for the toyshop door. A bell jangled and Christiana glimpsed a woman wearing a headscarf going inside, closing the door.

Gently, Jason eased her into the shadows of a darkened doorway and his breath came warm on her cheek as he bent lower. 'She probably thought we were lovers. Why don't we pretend we are? Kiss me, darling.'

'I wanted to talk to you!' she cried, flinging out her arms. 'Oh, I should have known this would happen. I must have been crazy to think we could talk calmly.'

He took a long, deep breath, his eyes glinting in the twilight. 'About what? For God's sake, you might as well tell me now and get it over with. What's eating you?'

'What you're doing at Deverill's, that's what! What are you up to, Jason? Are you deliberately making trouble?'

He straightened abruptly, as if she had hit him. 'What's that supposed to mean?'

'You know what it means. You've surely been aware of the rumours. There's been trouble at Deverill's ever since you arrived. There was the fire, and then an accident nearly injured my father. Now there's talk of a strike.

Tell me the truth, Jason—are you trying to get Deverill's shut down?'

'You can stand there and ask me that, after—'

'I had to ask,' she said desperately. 'I've got to know. People are saying all kinds of things about you. I only want you to tell me that none of it's true.'

He leaned towards her threateningly, his hands curling into fists. 'I refuse to dignify such an allegation with a denial! You can believe what you want to believe. And you say you're in love with me? You don't know how to love, Chris. You've no idea what the word means. But I'm grateful. You've finally made me see things clearly. If there's one thing Dee would never do it's believe lies about me.'

Swinging on his heel, he strode away, swift, ground-eating strides taking him rapidly up the hill to where lights shone from shops and houses.

'Jason!' Christiana shouted after him in despair, though she knew it was useless. 'But I don't believe it,' she moaned to herself. 'I only wanted to tell you what they were saying. I wanted to warn you. If you hadn't made me lose my temper . . .'

That Sunday evening, Christiana was at Arnside House alone, her parents having gone to spend the evening with her aunt and uncle.

When the phone rang she answered it without qualms; no sixth sense warned her what lay ahead.

'May I speak to Mr Deverill?' an unfamiliar male voice asked.

'I'm afraid he's out,' she replied. 'I'm his daughter. May I take a message?'

'Perhaps you can help me, Miss Deverill. This is the police. I understand a Mr Jason Straker is a colleague of your father's.'

'Yes, that's right.' Now, belatedly, her sixth sense came into play, sending a chill of apprehension through her. The voice sounded grave. 'What's happened?'

'I'm afraid there's been an accident,' came the reply. 'We were wondering if you know where we can contact any next of kin of Mr Straker, or of a Miss Debra Sloan.'

'What sort of accident?' she asked sharply. 'Are they hurt?'

'I'm afraid so. It's too early for me to go into details, particularly before we've informed their relatives. Do you happen to know—'

'There's no one. They're both from the States. But I'm a friend of theirs. Can't you tell me anything? Were they in a car?'

'They ran off the road, apparently,' the voice informed her. 'The car must have rolled several times.'

'And what about Jason and Dee?'

'Miss Sloan has cuts and abrasions, but she's comfortable. She's unable to help us at the moment because she's under sedation. Shock, you know.'

Was he deliberately trying to torture her, or was he trying to break bad news gently? Feeling as though her heart had stopped, she whispered, 'And Jason?'

'He's still unconscious, I'm afraid, but I'm sure the doctors are doing all they can for him. Are you certain there isn't anyone we can contact?'

'Well, of course there is! There's his family in America. But I don't know how to reach them. Look, I'll phone my father. He'll know what to do. Can you tell me . . . how badly is Mr Straker hurt? It's not serious, is it? He's not going—'

'I'm afraid that's all I know, Miss Deverill,' the man replied. 'Yes, if you'd get your father to contact us I'd be grateful. And try not to worry. I'm sure they'll do everything that's possible.'

She phoned her uncle's house and spoke to her father, hearing him tell her not to worry, that he would handle it. Then as soon as she put the phone down she ran out and flung herself into her car, taking it at speed along the dale and into Medfordham.

The hospital reception area was bright and modern. A few people waited there, one boy in a wheelchair with his sock off and a blue swelling at his ankle, his parents anxiously standing by; another young man with a bandaged hand, a woman with a dressing over her eye. The receptionist listened to

Christiana's enquiries, looked at her admissions' register and asked Christiana to take a seat.

Nurses came and went. A doctor came and fetched the boy in the wheelchair, taking him into an examination room. After a while he emerged and the family went off towards X-ray. Outside, an ambulance arrived with lights flashing, delivering its patient to a nearby door. A flurry of activity commenced.

To her relief, her father came through the door, a swift frown furrowing his brow as he saw her.

'What are you doing here, Chris?' he asked in an angry undertone. 'You ought to know better. Haven't you made enough of a fool of yourself already? He's not your concern. He has a fiancée. For goodness' sake, go home. Your mother's there. I dropped her off on the way.'

Christiana's mouth worked. He was right, of course. She hadn't thought how it would look, her rushing here and making a scene over Jason. 'I had to come,' she said, tears hot in her eyes. 'I've got to know how he is, Dad.'

He took her arm, hustling her into a corner away from curious eyes. 'I do understand, but now is not the time to forget discretion. I'll find out what's happening. As soon as there's any news I'll phone, I promise. But, please, Chris, go home and look after your mother.' He half-turned away, but looked back as a thought occurred to him. 'Did you contact Mrs Firestone?'

Christiana stared blankly at him, too upset to think.

'Dee's nurse,' her father amplified. 'She wasn't with them, was she?'

'I don't know,' she said. 'They didn't mention anyone else. I never thought about calling the hotel. He said next of kin.'

Her father rubbed her shoulder and leaned to kiss her cheek consolingly. 'All right, love. I'll see to it. I can see you're upset. Better get a taxi. Don't try driving while you're in this state.'

From behind him, the receptionist called, 'Miss Deverill?' But her father prevented her from answering the summons.

'I'll go. You get yourself home, love. I'll phone as soon as I know anything. And try not to worry.'

She returned to her car and, despite her father's warnings, drove herself home, though afterwards she remembered nothing about the journey. Her father had been wise, she supposed. Jason Straker was no concern of hers, except that if anything happened to him she would want to die.

'Has Dad phoned?' she asked as she rushed into Arnside House and found her mother waiting.

'No, not yet,' Mrs Deverill said with a sigh. 'Oh, Chris, we guessed you'd gone to the hospital. You really shouldn't have done that. It wasn't . . .'

'Discreet?' Christiana croaked. 'No, it wasn't. Could you be discreet if the man you loved was lying in hospital, probably dying, and nobody would tell you anything?'

Her mother regarded her with gentle sympathy. 'No, I couldn't. But, darling, the man you love belongs to another girl and it's time you accepted that. It's Dee you should be thinking about. Whatever will she do if she loses Jason?'

I don't care about Dee, she thought wildly, flinging her hands to her head, but it wasn't true—of course she cared about Dee.

If only Jason could recover his health and strength she would doggedly pretend she was happy for him and Dee, whatever happened, even if she had to keep up the charade for the rest of her life.

At last the phone rang and when she grabbed it up she found herself talking to her father.

'It's not quite so bad as you imagined,' he assured her. 'Jason's still unconscious but he's not on the critical list. They won't know much more until he comes round. As for Dee, she's shaken and shocked more than anything. They'll keep her in for a day or two, just to be sure.'

Somehow she found her voice, though it sounded unnatural. 'I see. I see. Thank God.'

‘I’m coming home now,’ her father added. ‘I’ll get in touch with the Strakers from Arnside House.’

He did so. Jason’s mother said she and her other son, and her daughter, would take the next flight out. Mr Deverill promised to meet them at the airport.

She was going to meet Jason’s family at last, Christiana thought sadly. In her wildest dreams she had never imagined it happening like this.

The following day, Christiana was astonished to receive a phone call from Dee Sloan, asking if she would go to see her at the Grand Hotel.

‘But how are you?’ Christiana asked in surprise. ‘I thought you were staying in hospital for a few days.’

‘I discharged myself,’ Dee replied. ‘I’ve got my nurse here to look after me. Please, Chris, come over here as soon as you can. We’ve got to talk.’

‘About what?’ Christiana asked, but the line had gone dead.

What could Dee possibly want? Christiana tried to guess from what she remembered of Dee’s tone, but no answers presented themselves.

She drove to the hotel in a state of perplexed apprehension and found Dee again ensconced on the settee with the faithful nurse in attendance. Bandages showed beneath the sleeve of Dee's slim-fitting woollen dress, and there was a slight scratch on her cheek; otherwise she showed no ill effects from the accident, though Christiana wondered if that careful make-up covered a paler-than-usual complexion.

'Sit down, Chris,' Dee invited, gesturing to a chair which had been drawn up near where she lounged on cushions.

Christiana sat, and said, 'How are you feeling? You ought to have stayed in hospital, you know. After a shock like that!'

'Oh, I'm OK,' Dee dismissed her concern. 'Like I said, I do have Bessie with me and she's a trained nurse. It's Jason I'm worried about. He hasn't come out of that coma yet. But you probably know that.'

'Yes.' She tried not to reveal how worried she was about Jason. 'My father called the hospital at lunchtime. It's terrible, Dee. Whatever happened?'

Dee exchanged a glance with the watchful nurse, who was busy doing unnecessary tidying of the room, her ears obviously wide open to catch every word of the conversation. When Dee looked again at Christiana her blue eyes were clouded with what might have been sympathy.

'You may as well know, Chris, he wasn't watching the road. There was a tractor coming. He didn't see it. We . . . we were too busy talking about . . . Well, I guess you know what we were discussing, don't you?'

Christiana felt the skin on her face tighten and knew the colour had drained from her cheeks. Dee had found out about the relationship between Jason and herself.

Not changing her expression of sorrowful understanding, Dee said quietly, 'He told me, Chris. He told me all about it.'

'I see.' She glanced down at the hands clenched round the strap of her shoulder bag, suddenly feeling mean and soiled.

'I told him, if he wanted, we could call off the wedding,' Dee's voice went on, every word driving Christiana further into shame. 'But he said it wasn't what he wanted. I'm sorry, Chris, but he only got mixed up with you because I wasn't here. I can understand that. He was lonely. You know how a man can get. He's very sorry that he hurt you—he told me so. But it was just one of those things.'

Christiana couldn't speak. She had never felt so empty and humiliated in her life.

'All I ask is that you won't try to see him again,' Dee went on. 'He's made his choice. Don't make difficulties for him. You'll do that for me, won't you? And if he should ever try to get in touch with you, I want you to turn him away. He's just a man and men don't always do what's right. I'm prepared to forgive and forget—this time. But another time I won't be so understanding—with him, or with you. Do you follow me?'

‘Yes,’ Christiana managed to say, lifting her head to look at Jason’s future wife. ‘And, Dee . . . I’m sorry.’ It seemed an inadequate thing to say but she could think of nothing else. She might have excused herself by saying that Jason had failed to mention his engagement until it was too late, but she couldn’t let him down like that, even though he had betrayed her by telling Dee the truth.

Christiana left, without even looking at Dee. Why had Jason felt obliged to tell Dee about it, at this late stage? To clear his conscience? Had they been arguing when the car went off the road? If so, then she was to blame for the accident and if Jason should be permanently injured in some way because of it, she would never forgive herself.

* * *

Jason and his family, with Dee and her nurse, flew back to the States on the day before Christmas Eve.

Although the weather was unseasonably mild, Christiana had never known a bleaker Christmas.

CHAPTER EIGHT

Leon Reynolds was forty-seven years old, of medium height with greying dark hair and a well-preserved body which he was currently showing off in swimming trunks as he dived cleanly from the springboard into the azure waters of the pool. Watching him, Christiana wondered if she should accept his proposal.

Maybe she had been mad to come with him to the Bahamas, but his quiet understanding had been a balm to her shattered heart. He knew what grief felt like, after all, having lost his wife only four months ago.

Only last night she had finally told Leon all about Jason Straker. Leon had listened, letting her pour out the whole story.

'I'm in the same boat, Chris, more or less. Losing Peg so suddenly last year was a terrible blow. But you've got to pick up the pieces and go on. There'll be someone else, in time.'

'No, I don't think so,' she had replied with a little shudder. 'I don't ever want to risk being hurt like that again.'

Leon had taken her hand gently in his. 'Then, if you mean that, why don't you and I team up? We get on well together, Chris. We could help each other forget the past. I've no one else to consider. Peg and I weren't lucky enough to have children. Everything I have can be yours. And everything I have is considerable.'

'I don't want your money, Leon,' she had said softly.

'I know. Maybe that's why I'm willing to offer it.'

He had left it at that, giving her time to think it over. He hadn't even tried to kiss her good-night before they went to their separate rooms. Now, in the heat of a February morning, she was still thinking about the proposition.

Leon was kind, considerate, generous, and if he was less than exciting at least he was steady. If she married him, she would be able to trust him, which was more than she could have said about Jason Straker.

Jason . . . The wound was still fresh and bleeding. She hadn't even seen him since they parted on that cold day with bitter words between them. The last news she had, via her father who had spoken on the phone with Mrs Straker, was that Jason was almost fully recovered from the accident and that the wedding was scheduled for January twenty-third.

That was a month ago. By now he and Dee were probably back from their honeymoon and planning their move to England, assuming they were coming back.

Since she left Yorkshire three weeks ago there had been no news; she had simply told her parents she was going away, not where or with whom, and the postcards she had sent home had been deliberately vague. If they had known she was staying with Leon Reynolds they might have been worried, fearing that unhappiness had driven her into a mad affair with the first man who came along.

The thought made her smile to herself as she lay with her eyes closed soaking up the sun. So far, her relationship with Leon could not have been more innocent.

'Let's have a drink,' Leon said. 'Have a drink and forget Jason, Chris. All he ever did was make you miserable.'

However, forgetting was something she was incapable of as yet. Her memories of Jason remained too fresh.

Her conversation with Leon disturbed her so much that, later that day, she phoned home to see if all was well.

'We're both fine,' her mother assured her. 'But how about you, darling? I could hardly believe my eyes when I got your first card. The Bahamas! Are you having a good time?'

'Fabulous,' Christiana said, overstating the case. 'I've developed the most marvellous tan and I feel much better. But how are things really? No problem at the factory?'

Her mother hesitated, then said with a sigh, 'I suppose you might as well know—they've called a strike starting next Monday.'

Christiana's heart sank. 'Oh, no! Why?'

'Something to do with the time-schedules, though you know your father doesn't tell me details. He's worried to death. Still, there's nothing you can do about it. I expect they'll sort this out. Dad has sent for Jason. He should be arriving any day now. If anyone can calm the shop stewards down, it's him. He can be charming when he tries, as you know all too well. Darling, are you really feeling better? You're not brooding?'

'Not all the time,' Christiana said, though that again was a prevarication. There were odd moments when she forgot her heartache, but they were few and far between.

'Are you on your own?' her mother asked.

Now it was Christiana who hesitated, but she had never been one to tell lies to her parents. She said, 'No. I'm with someone.'

'Another girl?'

'No.'

'Ah. I thought perhaps that might be the way of things. But, Chris, don't do anything foolish, will you? Whatever you may be thinking now, broken hearts do mend. Give it time, darling.'

'I will,' Christiana promised and, conscious of the cost of the call, ended the conversation with promises to be home in a week or so.

In the coolness of the villa with its arched rooms and white decor, she sat trying to imagine what it would be like to go home and know that Jason was nearby.

They lingered at the villa for another week

before taking the boat back to Nassau, in good time for their flight. Leon took her into the busy city with its skyscrapers and its parks of waving palm trees, and she found herself being coerced into a jeweller's shop where Leon had her look at trays of glittering rings.

'Leon . . .' She sighed.

'I know . . .' He cut her off before she could voice her protests. 'But I want to give you a present, anyway. You can wear it on your right hand for now. It's just a token of my affection, to remind you that I'm there in spirit if not in flesh.'

He brushed aside all her objections and when she refused to make a choice he chose for her—a massive solitaire diamond which flashed rainbows in the sunlight. She wore it on her right hand, regarding it as an amulet, a protection against memories of Jason Straker.

After the heat of the Bahamas, the cold of London in mid-February came as a shock.

Driving home the next day, she kept the diamond ring in its box, intending to break the news gently to her parents. Yorkshire looked wet and dark, with snow whitening the higher hills and lying in the hollows.

She arrived home mid-evening, to be greeted with warmth and affection by her parents. She had brought gifts for them, and for herself a shell to remind her of the Bahamas. It had white spikes and a pink interior, where faint murmurs of that blue ocean lingered.

Sitting talking with her parents, she described the islands and the things she had seen and done. Inevitably, Leon's name came into the discourse, though at first her parents made no comment.

Eventually, when the main thread of her story was ending, her mother said, 'So his name's Leon, is it? What's he like, Chris?'

'He's the nicest man I've ever known,' she replied, and it was the truth. Nice, relaxing, comfortable, all the adjectives she could never have applied to Jason. 'He's a widower—he lost his wife last year. I must have mentioned them to you—Leon and Peg?'

'Oh, that Leon!' her mother exclaimed, a worried look in her eyes. 'But I always had the impression he was older. Much older than you.'

'He is,' Christiana admitted with a glance at her father, who was listening but saying nothing. 'He's only five years younger than Dad. But he's lonely, too, and he couldn't have been kinder. He gave me a wonderful holiday. And, if you're interested, we didn't sleep together, it's not that sort of relationship. It's just . . . companionable, for both of us.'

This news didn't seem to be much consolation to her mother, and her father was tight-lipped.

Knowing she had to be completely honest, and it might as well be now as later, Christiana dug into her handbag for the ring box, and displayed the diamond for them to see. 'He bought me this. I'll be wearing it on my right hand. For now, anyway. Later on, well, we'll see how it goes. It's too soon for either of us to make big decisions.' Leave it at that, her subconscious told her. She put the ring away, and with it the subject of Leon, bracing herself for the news she had to hear sooner or later—news about Jason. 'So . . . what's happening about the strike?'

'It's still on, but at least we're negotiating,' her father said, seeming relieved to be back on firm conversational ground. 'I think they're beginning to see that Jason does know what he's doing. In time, the company will benefit all round from the changes he's made.'

'He's still totally committed, then?' she asked. 'He's not talking of pulling out?'

Her father frowned. 'Pulling out? What gave you that idea? No, of course he's not pulling out. He's totally committed to Deverill's. It'd take more than a temporary emotional hiccup for him to break the ties now.'

Stricken, Christiana looked down at her hands. That Jason might desert the company because of what had happened between her and him had been the last thing on her mind. She was relieved to know that Jason was not about to defect and leave Deverill's on the verge of bankruptcy.

Soon afterwards she excused herself on grounds of tiredness caused by jet-lag and she went to bed, to lie thinking sadly about Jason. 'A temporary emotional hiccup,' her father had called it. Was that what it had been to Jason, when to her it had been an earthquake which had split her to the foundations?

* * *

Christiana resumed her usual routine of work, plunging into it with a determination designed to make her forget that memories of Jason were everywhere in the studio.

Her father's birthday being due in March, she drove the icy roads into Harrogate one day and browsed round the shops looking for something suitable as a gift. She found herself in a big department store among handbags, scarves and displays of costume jewellery. Perfume from the nearby cosmetics department hung in the air as she paused to study some expensive leather driving gloves. Her father needed some new ones. Perhaps he would appreciate a pair of these, along with a bottle of the luxury aftershave which was being advertised only a few yards away. She sighed to herself, knowing she was being unimaginative.

Then some sixth sense made her look up, aware of being observed. From the other side of the shop fitment, behind a display of ladies' hats and scarves, Jason stood watching her.

Jason!

The sight of him seemed to rob her of the power of movement. How many times she had imagined this meeting, but it had never been like this, so unexpectedly and so far from familiar surroundings.

He stood watching her without expression, his face still and those green eyes holding a spark of challenge. He was wearing the many-pocketed green jacket he had had on when they last met, in Welmond, on the dreadful day when carols had hung in the air.

'Can I help you?' the voice of an assistant asked at her elbow. 'Would you like to buy those gloves?'

Christiana had forgotten she was still holding the gloves—she had almost put them in her pocket. The woman's tone sounded cold, as if she suspected Christiana of attempted shoplifting. Humiliated and embarrassed, Christiana decided, 'Yes, I'll have them. Thank you.'

'There's a cash point over here, if you'll follow me.' The assistant's attitude made it clear that she still had her doubts about her customer's honesty.

'I was miles away,' Christiana tried to explain. 'It's my father's birthday soon. I was trying to decide whether gloves would be a good idea.' She fumbled with her purse, extracting pound notes.

The driving gloves went into a paper bag, her money into the till. She turned away, trying not to look if Jason was still there.

'Your gloves!' the assistant exclaimed. 'Don't go without them.'

'Oh, yes, thank you.' Feeling an utter fool, she thrust the purchase into her shopping bag and began to walk away, only to catch a glimpse from the corner of her eye, of a familiar, many-zipped green jacket on a tall form walking directly towards her. Knowing she couldn't avoid a confrontation, she lifted her head and faced him levelly.

'Hello, Jason.'

'Hello, Chris,' he returned, matching her tone. 'Having problems?'

So he had witnessed that stupid episode of the gloves. 'No, not really. Just a bit absent-minded.' Be natural, she advised herself. Take a deep breath and be casual about this. 'Well, how are you?'

'Ninety per cent fit,' he replied.

Her brow creased in a frown she couldn't prevent. 'Only ninety per cent?'

'I still get blinding headaches occasionally, though they tell me they'll go away with time.'

'I'm sorry.' Could he see how worried she was about those headaches? But it wasn't her concern any more. He had renounced his relationship with her. He was married now. Married to Dee.

'What about you?' he asked. 'You're looking

good. That tan didn't come out of a bottle.'

'No. No, I've been away. The Bahamas, actually.'

His lips tightened. 'So I heard.' Judging by his expression, he had heard a good deal more than that. His glance slid to her hand, where the diamond winked in the bright lighting of the store. 'I gather congratulations are in order.'

'Who told you that?' It sounded sharper than she intended. 'If you'll take another look, I'm wearing this ring on my right hand, not my left.'

'You mean that makes a difference?' he asked with barely disguised sarcasm.

Now she was rattled, on the defensive and ready to strike. 'And how's Dee?' she asked in a brittle voice, reminding him that he had no right to question her private life. 'I gather she didn't come over with you.'

'No, she didn't.' The reply came matter-of-fact, but she fancied that the glint in his eye was caused by anger—anger directed at her. 'As it happens, there were some delayed complications from the accident.'

Christiana caught her breath. 'I'm sorry to hear that. She ought to have stayed in hospital a bit longer, instead of discharging herself. I hope it's nothing serious.'

'No, it's not.' He was still looking at her with a grim set to his mouth which she found impossible to interpret.

Affecting lightness, as if he were just another acquaintance, she said, 'What are you doing in Harrogate, anyway? I certainly didn't expect to run into you here.'

'No, I guess you didn't,' he said tightly. 'If you'd known I'd be here for a business meeting you'd have avoided the place like the plague, I know. You don't have to spell it out, Chris. I've got the message loud and clear.'

She glanced around her, at other customers wandering about examining goods. One couple had paused to stare at her and Jason, much to her embarrassment.

'Keep your voice down,' she muttered.

He did lower his voice, but the glint in his eyes had flared into fury as he said under his breath, 'I guess it's terribly British to stand here and make polite conversation. But you'll forgive me if I don't play your game any longer. If I stay around for another minute I may very well give in to the temptation to wring your beautiful neck!'

With which he pushed forcibly past her, almost knocking her over as he strode rapidly away.

When she arrived home, she phoned Leon and asked him to come up to Yorkshire the following weekend. He would help her keep up the pretence, she knew. He was her smoke screen, her protection from the gossips. But she didn't tell him she had seen Jason. That was something she could never tell anyone. All the wounds had opened again, just as deep and painful as before.

CHAPTER NINE

Christiana's parents pretended to be pleased that Leon was coming, though Christiana knew they had reservations about her relationship with an older man, especially when that relationship had begun so soon after her involvement with Jason ended. But if she was on the rebound, then so was Leon; they had talked about it several times!

Leon arrived on Friday evening and the four of them spent an uneasy few hours making stilted conversation, except when the two men got on to business matters. Both owned companies which were having industrial troubles, so at least on that subject they could converse as equals.

'He seems very nice,' her mother commented as they made coffee in the kitchen late that night. 'A bit . . . opinionated, perhaps.'

Christiana had never thought of Leon in that way, but she supposed her mother was right. She had seen her father biting his tongue several times rather than disagree with a guest. It wasn't going very well.

'He's a bit tense,' she said in Leon's defence. 'I mean, he knows he's not your idea of the perfect son-in-law. He's trying too hard to make a good impression. But he's kind, Mum. Give him time to settle down with us.'

*　　*　　*

In the morning, Leon was more his usual self, especially after Mr Deverill had gone off for his usual Saturday round of golf, despite the chill wet wind of the February day. Soon Leon and her mother were on first-name terms, and chatting happily about their childhood experiences during the war.

'This is terrible,' Leon said eventually. 'It must sound like ancient history to Chris. But it was an exciting time, wasn't it, Gwen?'

'It had its moments,' Mrs Deverill replied. 'I don't think I really understood what was happening. But, look, I have to make a start on lunch. You two go off and have some time together. I mustn't monopolise you, Leon. You're here to see Chris.'

Smiling, he let his glance slide over Christiana in her slim slacks and chunky sweater. 'And isn't she a sight for sore eyes? You have a lovely daughter, Gwen. And now I know where she got her looks from.'

That pleased her mother, Christiana could see, though Mrs Deverill laughed off the compliment and said she was much too fat and middle-aged to stand comparison with her daughter.

Christiana took Leon to show him her study, where her design ideas came to fruition. He was interested to see her working surroundings, and impressed by the designs on which she was currently engaged.

'You have a natural flair,' he told her, standing by her drawing board. 'I think I'll offer you an exclusive contract rather than sharing your talent with other companies. I mean to say, I can't have my girl working for the opposition, now, can I?'

He was quite serious, she realised, not knowing whether to be flattered or intimidated. It was as though he had shown her the door of a cage and invited her to step inside, which was irrational . . .

On Sunday morning, when Christiana and her mother were busy preparing a traditional roast with all the trimmings, Mr Deverill offered to show Leon round his works. Leon eagerly accepted, though Christiana wondered what lay behind the invitation. Perhaps her father wanted to have a heart-to-heart discussion with his prospective son-in-law.

The two men were late for lunch, much to the annoyance of Christiana and her mother, but when finally the pair returned they were so full of apologies that they were forgiven. Besides, they had good news; they had run into Jason, who was fresh from an informal meeting with the shop stewards to negotiate a new deal over the ending of the strike.

'They'd all been to the club to chat over a few drinks,' Mr Deverill informed his wife and daughter over lunch. 'Jason didn't tell me about it in advance in case nothing came of it, but it looks as though he's finally won them over. After we all meet tomorrow, the strike will be called off, thank God.'

Leon said nothing, not then, but his silence seemed to Christiana to be a symptom of grave doubts. But she was busy after lunch helping with the dishes and clearing up the kitchen, so she didn't have a chance of talking with him privately until he was on the point of leaving.

His overnight bag stood by the door as they paused in the hall to say final good-byes, with her parents discreetly behind the closed door of the sitting-room.

'Do I gather you're not so impressed as Dad over Jason's victory?' Christiana asked, straightening the lapels of his car coat.

'Oh, he's a miracle worker,' Leon replied sourly. 'No doubt about it. Saved the day. How very convenient! A whitewash job if ever I saw one.'

A heavy sigh escaped her. 'You could be wrong, you know. You're bound to be a bit prejudiced.'

'Let's just say he confirmed my worst fears. I don't trust him an inch, and I'm not at all happy about leaving you here where he can get to you. Please, Chris, make up your mind and come to me. I meant what I said about that exclusive contract. There'll be no worries about somewhere to live, since I've already got my house. Just pack your bags and come, as soon as possible. Please!'

'You mean . . . live with you?' she queried.

Leon laid his hands on her waist, gazing anxiously into her eyes. 'At first, yes. We can get married any time. Look, I know you still feel something for Straker, but do you really want to risk what could happen? He's not the type to give up easily. His wife isn't with him, is she? If he starts prowling round you again, will you be able to resist him?'

'He won't do that,' she said quietly. 'It's over between us, Leon. It's been over since last December.'

'Oh, has it? You think so? Well, I've had a lot more experience than you have and from what he said to me—' The sentence cut off and his eyes slid away from hers, as if he knew he had said too much. She had never seen him so agitated.

'Why, what did he say?' she asked. 'Something about me? In front of my father?'

Leon shrugged his shoulders uncomfortably, still unable to meet her glance. 'No. No, we had a few minutes alone. What we said to each other isn't important. It was mainly the feeling I got. Hostility poured out of him.' At last he looked at her, his blue eyes clouded and anxious. 'He's jealous, Chris. And if that's how he feels then it's not over between you, not by a long chalk.'

* * *

The following morning, Christiana was in her studio trying to force her mind into a state which would allow her to work. But her thoughts kept straying to what might lie ahead for her, to go and live with Leon or to stay at Arnside House and risk further entanglement with Jason.

Without warning, her mother burst into the studio, beaming, carrying a huge bouquet of red roses. 'Look what's come, Chris. Aren't they gorgeous? They must be from Leon.' She laid the flowers across the drawing board, extracting a small envelope. 'Here's the card, look. Shall I put them in water for you? All in one vase, or shall I split them? You could have some in here and some in the sitting-room.'

'Yes, that sounds like a good idea,' Christiana said vaguely.

'Which does? All together, or split them?'

'Split them, if you don't mind.'

'No, I'll enjoy arranging them. I love roses. They must have cost the earth. Isn't it nice of him to think of sending flowers?'

'Leon is nice,' Christiana said, and her mother took the roses away.

She opened the card idly, not really interested in what message Leon had sent, but the sight of the handwriting on the card struck her like a physical blow. Black, jagged, it sprawled across the card arrogantly. She had seen that handwriting before, in dim light at the Mayor's Ball, scrawled across a notebook. Jason's handwriting!

What it said was, *Happy Anniversary*. Just that, with no signature, not even an initial. But she knew who had sent it—and the roses.

Anniversary, she thought, casting her mind back. Anniversary of what? Their last meeting? No, it couldn't be. What was he trying to do? Was this the start of the 'prowling' Leon had warned her about? Was he out of his mind to risk sending roses to her now that he was married? When she had last seen him he had threatened to wring her neck. Were the roses meant to torment her?

She couldn't make sense of it. All she knew was that the arrival of the roses disturbed her more than she would have thought possible. Thank heaven her mother had assumed they came from Leon. Everyone could just go right on making the same assumption.

She and her mother were having lunch when a phone call from Brian Fleming took Christiana into the hall.

'I wonder if you felt like playing badminton tonight?' Brian asked. 'It's ages since I saw you. You don't think your new boy friend would object to your spending an hour with an old friend, do you?'

'No, I'm sure he wouldn't,' Christiana replied. 'Do you know, that's just what I feel like—a good workout. Thanks, Brian. Will you book the court? Shall I meet you at the sports centre?'

'Oh . . . no, don't let's use two lots of petrol. I'll pick you up about seven. And, Chris, you might like to know that the meeting with the strike committee has just finished. It's settled at last. Everything looks good for Deverill's.'

She let out a breath of relief. 'That's good news, Brian. Thanks, I'll tell Mother we've weathered the storm.'

'It was all thanks to Mr Straker, you know,' Brian said confidentially. 'It looks as though I was wrong about him. I suppose you heard they caught the chap that started that fire?'

'No! When was this?'

'Just after you went flying off to Barbados, or wherever it was. It was a man your father sacked for stealing two or three years ago. Apparently, since then his luck's gone from bad to worse, and he blamed Deverill's for it. So it didn't have any connection with Mr Straker.'

'I never believed that it did,' she said flatly. 'Well, I wish someone had told me before, but I suppose they forgot I didn't know about it. Remind me to give you a lecture tonight about jumping to conclusions. As an accountant, you ought to know that two and two don't make five.'

'OK, point taken. I'm sorry if I made things more difficult for you, but I was genuinely worried. I suppose I'm just a naturally suspicious character. But I must get back to work. 'Bye, Chris. See you tonight.'

'I'll look forward to it,' she said, putting the phone down. A game of badminton was just what she needed to get rid of some of the tension inside her. It might also prevent her from telling Brian just what she thought of him and his super-suspicious mind.

But a moment later she forgot all about Brian because as she returned to the kitchen to finish her lunch, her eye fell on the calendar, which declared that today was the first of March. And last year, she remembered, had been a leap year, so a year ago today had been February twenty-ninth. Now she knew what anniversary the roses commemorated. Exactly a year ago today, she and Jason had met for the very first time.

* * *

That evening, there was snow on the ground and more in the wind as she watched for Brian's arrival, with her sports gear in a bag and her badminton racquet in its cover. Seeing lights come up the drive, she called good-bye to her parents and went out into the cold wind, shivering closer into her anorak hood as she ran for the familiar car whose racy shape was emphasised by two white lines running along its flank.

He leaned to open the door for her, taking her bag and racquet and tossing them on to the back seat as she dropped into the car beside him and slammed the door, throwing back her hood. The car eased forward at once.

'Whew! It's cold,' she remarked, pulling the seat belt across and looking for the locking fitment.

Then—and only then—did she notice the zipped pockets on the sleeve of the driver's jacket. For a second she froze, twisted round in her seat, not believing what her senses told her. Jason had a jacket just like that.

Her eyes jerked to the sturdy profile visible in the light from the dashboard, and she found she could hardly breathe, let alone speak.

'Well, fasten it,' Jason said tightly, watching the road.

By dint of swallowing hard and painfully, she managed to say, 'What's going on?'

He flashed her a glance and even in the half-light she could see he was angry. 'Fasten the belt, Chris!'

She did so, her thoughts in disarray as she settled more comfortably in her seat. 'I demand to know what's going on! What are you doing with Brian's car?'

'He lent it to me,' he said with another furious glance at her. 'We're going for a little drive, you and I.'

This could not be happening, she thought wildly. 'Are you out of your mind? Turn this car round. I'm not going anywhere with you. It was a plot, wasn't it? You and Brian planned this.'

She saw his muscular thigh jerk as he slammed on the brake so hard that the car slid momentarily in the slush on the road. When it stopped, he left the engine running as he turned to her and said in a soft, menacing voice, 'You're coming with me, Miss Deverill, whether you like it or not. I warn you, I've got a lousy headache and I'm in a filthy mood. If I have any more hassle from you I won't answer for the consequences. Just sit still and button your lip, at least until we get where we're going. You hear?'

'I hear,' she said stiffly. 'But if you think—'

A none-too-gentle hand fastening on her jaw stopped her. 'I said be quiet, Chris. You'll have a chance to answer back later. Just for once in your life stop being so uppity and do as you're told.'

CHAPTER TEN

After a while, Christiana guessed they were heading for Jason's cottage. That was when she started to get alarmed. The further they climbed into the hills, the deeper lay the snow, covering the road now and being lashed in thick swathes across the windscreen. In the tunnel of the headlights, white flakes drove hard and furious.

'You do realise that if this weather keeps up, the roads will soon be blocked,' she said crisply.

'Too bad,' he replied.

'Jason! Look—please . . . What are you trying to prove? I honestly don't know what I've done to make you angry, but—'

He stopped her with a look, but immediately returned his attention to the road. 'You don't know,' he said with disgust. 'You really don't know, huh?'

'I really don't,' she repeated, trying to sound reasonable. 'Unless it's because of that day in Welmond. Honestly, Jason, I wasn't making accusations. It came out all wrong because I lost my temper. I never believed you were intentionally making trouble at work. I swear I didn't.'

'No? Not even for one tiny second? Of course you did, or you'd never have asked me about it. You listened to Brian Fleming, didn't you? Well, sure you did. The two of you were always pretty thick. Seems like I was for ever seeing the two of you together—at the Ball, at the sports centre, outside the works—kissing each other in public by the gates.'

'I never kissed Brian!' she denied. 'Well, not in public.'

'I saw you, dammit!'

She turned in her seat, saying hotly, 'What you saw was him kissing me, on the cheek, just in a friendly way. Anyhow, what business is it of yours? Jason, why are you doing this to me? If we get stuck out here, everyone will know about it by tomorrow morning. Maybe you don't care about my reputation, but if there's talk then Dee might hear it when she comes over. We can't do that to her.'

'It's a bit late to worry about Dee,' he said with another angry look. 'We were discussing you and Brian. You deny you led him on?'

That question made her draw back, puzzling over the strange circumstances by which he had accomplished this abduction. 'What has Brian been saying?'

'A lot of things. All of them mighty interesting. He and I seemed to be almost in the same boat. I mean to say, if you were going to take up with anyone it ought to have been Brian, oughtn't it?'

'Brian and I are friends, and that's all. He knows that as well as I do. If he's told you anything else—'

'Oh, he hasn't, don't worry. When we finally got around to talking about it, he set me right on that score. But I know all that hogwash about me and the company came via Brian because he told me so. He apologised for it. He and I are good buddies at long last.'

'Hence the car,' she deduced. 'You arranged this between you. The badminton was just a ploy.'

'Exactly.'

'So you knew you were going to kidnap me.'

'Honey,' said Jason softly, threateningly, 'you climbed in this car of your own volition. Don't make out I used force because I didn't. And I don't intend to. I may feel like throttling you, but I'll contain myself.'

Down the long, dale road the snow lay deep and unmarked, with more flying all the time to thicken the white blanket. It crunched beneath the car's wheels as Jason drove slowly round the curve and in between gateless posts to stop in front of the darkened cottage.

'I'm not coming in with you,' Christiana said flatly. 'Jason, this is crazy.'

He turned on her with bared teeth. 'Sure it's crazy. I'm crazy. You've driven me crazy. But stay out here if you want to freeze to death.'

Leaving the car, he took the keys with him, and moments later lights went on inside the cottage, glowing warmly through claret-coloured curtains. Christiana stayed where she was though the temperature inside the car dropped rapidly now that the heater was off.

Eventually, in a vile temper, she got out of the car and sank into snow well over the tops of her shoes. Already the tracks of the car were being filled in by fresh flakes that fell thick and fast.

She waded through drifts to a small glass porch which enclosed the cottage door. Inside the porch she stamped most of the snow from her feet and opened the farther door, intending to give Jason a piece of her mind.

Warmth met her, from a blazing fire in a big stone hearth across the room. A comfortable leather suite was arranged on a thick carpet patterned in claret and pine, while open-tread stairs climbed up from one corner, the banister hung with plants that trailed greenery. And in a chair by the fire, Jason sat rubbing the back of his neck as if he were in pain, his head bent.

She watched him worriedly, her temper fading.

'Jason, if we don't go back now we're going to get snowed in. My parents—they'll be worried—'

'You can phone them,' he muttered without looking up, his hands pressed round his head.

'And tell them I'm with you? Oh, won't that look great?'

'I hadn't reckoned on the snow,' he said

through clenched teeth.

Her feet were wet from melting snow and the fire looked inviting. Slowly, she moved across the room to stand on the hearthrug and hold her hands to the blaze, watching Jason with his head in his hands only two feet away.

'Is your headache very bad?' she asked with concern.

'It'll ease off soon. I took some pills.'

'Well, can I make you a hot drink? Or would it help if I massaged your neck?'

Lifting his head carefully, he gave her a look that derided her. If you massage my neck, his look said, what might it lead to?

Her own head felt as though it might burst. 'Please give me the car keys,' she begged. 'I'll drive myself back.'

'Not in this weather.'

'I'm a sight better driver than you are!' she exclaimed without thinking, and saw how that hurt him. He had driven off the road while quarrelling with Dee—quarrelling about her. 'I'm sorry, I didn't mean that. Jason, why did you bring me here? You know I can't stay. I understand why you were annoyed with me and I'm sorry I listened to Brian, even for a moment. But we've got to be sensible.'

'Why?'

'Because we must!'

'I guess it might help if you rubbed my neck,' he said.

He didn't seem to be listening, she thought

despairingly. Perhaps his headache was so bad he couldn't think straight.

Tossing off her anorak, she seated herself on the broad arm of the black leather chair in which he sat. Her fingers gently kneaded the knotted muscles at the top of his spine. She tried not to think about it, but being so near him torture. This was Jason, and she loved him, and he was in pain and needed her.

'That's good,' he muttered. 'Yes, there. Slow and easy.'

Distressed to the point of tears, she stopped the massage, leaving her hands resting against his shoulders where the firm warmth of him made the nerves in her fingers respond with a trembling delight that spread all through her.

He was leaning on his knees, his head in his hands. In a muffled voice, he said, 'Are you going to marry that Reynolds guy?'

Even though he couldn't see her, she shook her head, unable to speak for fear of betraying her distress. Her hands moved caressingly down his back.

'Well, are you?' Jason prompted gruffly.

Christiana straightened her spine, taking her hands away from him. 'No, I don't think so.'

He turned very slowly to look at her, his eyes bright with agony as he laid his hands on her waist.

'I promised Dee it wouldn't happen again,' she told him.

A frown creased between his brows, allied with a look of total bewilderment in his eyes. 'You did what?'

'I promised Dee,' she repeated.

'When?'

'It was the day after the accident, when we didn't know if you'd ever recover. Oh, love, if you knew how afraid I was for you. I made a bargain with God, that if you could get well I'd try to be content with things as they are. Then Dee asked me to go and see her and she told me she knew all about us. She wasn't nasty about it. She just asked me to leave you alone and I promised I would.'

His frown had deepened, as if he was baffled by what she was saying. 'She knew?' he queried. 'You didn't tell her about us?'

'I didn't need to—you'd already told her yourself.'

Jason lay back in the chair, his arm loosely around her waist as he tipped his head back and closed his eyes tightly. 'I told her?'

'So she said. That's what you were talking about when you had the accident.'

His eyes snapped open, blazing at her. 'And I suppose I've got to take your word for that, when I don't remember what the hell happened!'

With a suddenness that startled her, he wrenched himself to his feet and stood on the rug, a hand clawing through his hair as he stared down at the fire.

'It's not my word you have to accept,' she said quietly, wounded by his scepticism. 'I'm only repeating what Dee told me. Don't you believe me?'

'I don't know what to believe,' he muttered, holding his head.

Watching him worriedly, Christiana noticed the picture above the hearth. It was the tapestry picture of the old mill, for which he had out-bid her at the auction and which he had wanted her to take as a gift. 'You've still got that picture,' she said sadly.

'What picture?' He glanced at her, then up at the chimney breast. 'Oh, that one. Yes. I've got the other one, too.' Frowning blackly, he looked down at her across his shoulder. 'And don't change the subject.'

'I wasn't! Jason, will you please tell me what I've done?'

'You . . .' he began threateningly, and made a vicious gesture. 'You and that Reynolds guy! You sent him to get rid of me, didn't you? Sent him to buy me off?'

'What?' she said faintly. 'Whatever do you mean?'

He leaned over her, glowering. 'He came and offered to buy out my shares in Deverill's if I'd clear off and leave you alone. You should have seen the pompous ass! I nearly laid him out.'

'If he did any such thing,' Christiana said in a voice that shook, 'it certainly wasn't because

I sent him to do it. He did say . . . at least, he gave me the impression you'd had words.'

'Words!' With a sharp laugh he straightened. 'You can say that again!'

She leapt to her feet, her hands clenched at her sides. 'You think I asked him to do that? I didn't know a thing about it. You surely don't believe that I would—'

'No, of course I don't,' he broke in, turning away wearily.

'Then why say it?'

He swung round again. 'Because I was so flaming mad! To see him standing there defending you—against me! I could have killed him!'

'He did think,' she managed to say, 'that you seemed a bit jealous.'

'Well, it wouldn't take much brain to know that!' His hands shot out and fastened on her shoulders, jerking her towards him as his eyes fired with anguish. 'Of course I was jealous. Sick with it. You're mine, Chrissy. Mine!'

Before she could move, his mouth closed over hers with a hurting, angry passion that dismayed her. Momentarily she stiffened, knowing she ought to fight him off, but her own feelings broke the barrier of her control and she flung her arms round him, holding him tightly as that fierce kiss deepened. They pressed together urgently, months of agony and separation turning them both a little mad.

But eventually she buried her face in his shoulder.

'I'm not married to Dee. I'm not married full stop,' he said suddenly.

She became utterly still, not even breathing. Dear God, what had he said? Slowly she lifted her tear-stained face to search his eyes, where she saw that he was telling the truth.

'Say that again,' she said incredulously.

'I'm not married,' he repeated. 'Not married, not engaged, not tied in any way.'

Such relief flowed through her that she leaned weakly against him, her arms locked around him.

For what seemed a long time they stayed like that, holding each other, while Christiana finally allowed herself to believe the wondrous fact. He was free at last! Free to belong to her. For the first time she could be in his arms and not feel guilty, because now there was no one else between them.

'What happened?' she asked.

A long sigh breathed out of him. 'A lot,' he said, bending to kiss her caressingly once more before looking deep into her eyes. 'Chrissy, do you love me?'

'Don't you know?' she asked softly. 'I've always loved you. From the very first moment, a year ago.'

'Me, too,' he said, and bent his lips to hers again as if he had to keep reassuring himself she was his. He drew her in closer, cradling her head to his shoulder. 'I've been confused, I guess. Lately, nothing's happened the way it should.'

'That accident didn't help,' she told him. 'You were unconscious for three days. It takes time to recover properly from something like that. How's your headache?'

'Almost gone,' he assured her with a smile. 'They come and they go, getting less frequent all the time. Being uptight lately hasn't helped. Hopefully, now that you and I are together, the headaches will disappear. But come and sit down—we've got to talk.'

He poured some drinks and they sat on the big leather settee, his arm curled around her.

'Tell me about Dee,' she requested. 'You said there were complications after the accident. Is that why you didn't get married?'

A wry smile tugged at a corner of his mouth. 'Kind of. What happened was . . . About a week before the wedding was due, when I was still feeling groggy, we had a letter from the doctor in the hospital here. He thought we'd be interested to know that the man who witnessed the accident with the Porsche and called the ambulance, had seen Dee on her feet, staggering round the field.

'I guess the doctor had other things on his mind,' Jason went on, 'but he must have heard that Nurse Bessie collected Dee in a wheelchair. Anyway, he eventually got round to writing us about it. He wondered if Dee's paralysis might be psychosomatic.'

'And is it?'

He tilted an eyebrow at her sardonically. 'We had her see our own doctor, who confirmed there was no physical reason for her not being able to walk. He also said she'd got a lot of mobility back since the accident, though she hadn't let on to us.'

'But why? Heavens, if it had been me, I'd have been overjoyed!'

'Would you?' he asked with a cynical twist to his lips. 'Even if you had a rich fiancé you were desperate to hang on to? And when you suspected the only hold you had on him was through being helpless?'

'She knew that?' Poor Dee, she thought, unable to prevent a wave of sympathy for the girl. 'But I don't understand why your financial situation was relevant. I always assumed her people were on a par with yours. You said she was your sister's friend.'

'So she was, but she . . . Well, she came from the wrong side of the tracks, as they say. When she came over to our house she was like a kid in a toy-store. I guess I started out feeling sorry for her and just went right on feeling sorry for her. I was too stupid to know that sympathy isn't the same as love.'

'No, but it's very similar. You're not the first to have made that mistake. But what did you do when you discovered she wasn't permanently paralysed?'

Jason lifted her hand to kiss the slim fingers entwined with his. 'I called off the wedding. At first it was just a postponement, to see how she went on with psychiatric help, and then . . . Well, the shrink found out a couple of other things about Dee, mostly that she was terrified of a full, marital relationship.'

'But didn't you ever suspect it?' Christiana asked. 'You can't be engaged to someone and not know a thing like that.'

'You'd think so, yes,' Jason said drily. 'I did have a feeling something wasn't quite right, but I assumed it was her strict upbringing that made her hold me off. Then that last day we were here . . .' His voice trailed off as a frown creased his brow and he stared past her with narrowed eyes. 'We were here,' he repeated with surprise.

'I remember it now. I was in a terrible mood after that fight with you in Welmond. So I brought Dee here, just the two of us. She kept saying wait—wait until we're married. I remember asking her if it would be any different when we were married, and she said yes, of course it would. But I could see the panic in her eyes. She was scared stiff.'

After that revelation, the silence went on so long that Christiana cried, 'So what did you do about it?'

'Why—nothing. I packed her into the car and . . . Funny, it's all come back to me now. I knew by that time I couldn't marry her, however sorry I felt for her. I was beginning to realise that she saw me only as a ticket to the good life, and anyhow, I was too much in love with you to have gone on pretending any longer.

'I said something about delaying the wedding until she'd seen a doctor, because obviously she wasn't ready to be married to anybody the way she was. She got upset. She accused me of having another woman. Naturally I denied it—I wasn't going to have you dragged into it. But she said she knew there was someone, because she'd found that note in my wallet.' He glanced at her tight-lipped with remembered anger. 'She'd actually been through my wallet, would you believe? I was furious with her.

'Then there was something on the road . . . a tractor . . . she screamed . . . she grabbed the wheel . . . God, yes! She grabbed the wheel, the little fool! Why the hell couldn't I remember that before?'

Jason sat forward, leaning on his knees with his fingers in his hair. 'She knew I didn't remember what happened. She would have let me go through with the wedding without ever letting on to me that I'd had second thoughts. I knew there was something weird. In the back of my mind I knew it, but I was too groggy to understand. If we'd never heard from that doctor in Medfordham, by now . . . Hell, it makes my skin crawl to think of it.'

Turning to her, he took her hands in his, adding, 'But you see, sweetheart, I didn't tell her about you and me. When I finally called off the wedding for good, she turned nasty. She said she supposed I was going running back to you. I asked her why she thought you had anything to do with it and she said you had told her about us. You had told her we were lovers. You'd threatened a scandal if she didn't release me. Look, if it's true, it doesn't matter. You can tell me.'

'Can you see me doing anything of the kind?' Christiana asked. 'Me? It's true I did go to see her—but only because she sent for me. And then she informed me, very sweetly, that she knew all about it. You had told her you were sorry you ever got involved with me. "Just one of those things," I think she said. And she made me promise not to try to communicate with you again. I felt dreadful. The proverbial scarlet woman. Honestly, Jason, she said that you had told her . . .' The words trailed off as the scene in the hotel replayed in her mind.

'You've remembered something?' he prompted.

'I've realised something,' she said with a heavy sigh. 'She didn't know for sure, she only had suspicions. My reactions can only have confirmed those suspicions. I must have had guilt written all over me. So in a way I did tell her.'

Jason took her in his arms, kissing her

softly. 'All she was trying to do was to make you stay clear until she'd got me to the altar,' he surmised. 'If I'd seen you before we left, I might have remembered what really happened. As it was, I didn't know what the hell to think. After I cancelled the wedding, I went off for a convalescent trip to the mountains. On my own.'

'You did?' she murmured, touching his face.

'I did.' He was frowning again as he pulled free and stood up. 'But not until after I'd phoned to try and talk to you and discovered that you, my little English icicle, were off sunning yourself in the Bahamas. It was just great, busting to tell you the good news, and find out you were so upset at losing me that you'd run off with some other guy.'

'Of course I was upset. That's why I went.'

'With a guy old enough to be your father?' he demanded furiously.

Christiana jumped up, her own temper rising. 'What are you insinuating? It was purely platonic.'

'Oh, yeah? That's why you came back wearing his ring, is it? People couldn't wait to tell me about that. "She must be engaged," they said. "She's wearing this huge diamond!" '

'It is not—' she began loudly and calmed herself with an effort. 'I told you it wasn't an engagement ring, I told you that! Why didn't you tell me you weren't married? Just to torment me, I suppose. To see how miserable it made me. Do you realise that I was on the point of going to live with Leon, just because you had failed to inform me of that insignificant detail?'

Jason glared at her, full of rage. 'I'd never have allowed you to go and live with that superannuated ape! I'd have locked you up first.'

'Indeed?' she retorted, but her temper was subsiding at the sight of the fierce jealousy in him.

'And beaten you!' he added.

'Oh, really?'

'Really!' But the fight was seeping out of him, too, and a spark of amusement glimmered in the depths of his eyes.

'Jason!' She flew at him, torn between beating him and hugging him. Her arms fastened tightly round his neck as he enfolded her in a bear hug and their mouths met and fused in a long, passionate, aching kiss of joyful reunion.

'Hey, hold it,' Jason protested after a while, drawing back his head to look at her with a frown, though his eyes were laughing. 'Miss Deverill, are you throwing yourself at me?'

'Shamelessly,' she declared. 'Oh, you beast. You horrible, teasing, beautiful . . .' The words trailed off in his mouth as he kissed her again, releasing a flood of pleasure inside her . . .

'I love you, too, sweetheart,' he told her softly, deeply, as he bent to kiss her tenderly.

'I guess that puts paid to the icicle theory, anyhow. Miss Deverill, you're really something.'

'You're not so bad yourself,' she murmured, brushing her lips across his mouth.

She saw him smile to himself in pleasure at her touch.

'I never knew what love was before. I never came near to guessing, until I met you. It gives me the shivers how near I came to marrying Dee.'

'It doesn't bear thinking about,' she agreed, burrowing against him. 'Jason,' she whispered, lost in the wonder of him. 'Jason, I love you.'

* * *

'One thing I don't understand. What note did Dee find in your wallet? I never wrote you any notes.'

He took a wallet from the back pocket of his trousers. Out of it he extracted a sheet of folded notepaper which he gave to her.

By the light of the lamp, Christiana saw that it was the page from his notebook on which they had communicated at the Ball, his handwriting and hers contrasting with those flippant, cryptic messages which had been the first blossoms on the tree of their traumatic romance.

'You kept it?' she said softly. 'All this time?'

'It was all I had,' he reminded her, replacing

the paper safely in the corner of his wallet. 'All I had of that uppity little madam I fell in love with the first time I laid eyes on her.' A gentle finger traced the line of her profile down from her brow across her nose, to pause at her lips. 'I didn't know it then, but I guess that's what happened. You never really fooled me, you know. I always knew there was a warm female under all that British reserve. I just had a hard time finding her.'

'Well, you've found her now,' she murmured. 'Just don't ever let her go again.'

Over his shoulder, she glimpsed her picture of moonlight on water, which he had bought at the auction.

Following the line of her gaze, Jason smiled to himself. 'I told you you were a romantic, but you wouldn't have it. Now maybe you'll let me give you that tapestry I bought for you.'

'It looks good above your fireplace, though.'

'Oh, I don't intend to move it. I'll give you the wall it's hanging on, too. The whole cottage, in fact. And myself, if you'll have me.'

'If that's a proposal . . .' she murmured.

'It's a most urgent and sincere request,' he told her earnestly. 'Please marry me, Chrissy. Soon.'

'Very soon,' she promised. 'It's funny,' she said after a while. 'I sometimes used to think that if ever we got together it might finish what was between us. But it's not so, is it?'

'Sweetheart,' he said softly, 'if I live to be a hundred I can never have enough of you. We haven't finished, we've only just begun. And considering we've known each other a whole year already, I'd say we ought to try catching up on some lost time.'

'We will, now. Oh—I haven't thanked you for the roses. I thought you were crazy to send them, but now I understand. It was a year ago today, wasn't it? That night you first came to dinner at Arnside House. You weren't what I was expecting.'

'No?' His slow, teasing smile lit up his face. 'Well, neither were you, sweet. I guess we both got a surprise that night. But we've played it all wrong. You realise I've never taken you out on a date? Miss Deverill, will you have dinner with me tomorrow night?'

'Why, Mr Straker,' she replied archly, 'I thought you'd never ask.' Then a sudden thought struck her. 'At least, we'll go out to dinner if we can. Is it still snowing?'

'I'll take a look.' He pulled the curtain aside, glancing round after a moment to beckon her.

Christiana went slowly, drinking in the sight of him. He was still the most beautiful man she had ever seen. For her, he would always be the most beautiful man in the world.

The look on her face made him draw her into the curve of his arm and they kissed before he showed her what lay outside. The snow had almost covered Brian's car. Light from the cottage windows fell softly pink over the banks and drifts of perfect whiteness, and it was still snowing.

'They do have snow ploughs around here, I hope,' Jason said.

'Oh, yes, but, it could be two or three days before they get this far. We're so out in the wilds.'

He pulled a wry face and grinned at her. 'Wish you ere hack in the Bahamas? I bet it wasn't like this there.'

'No, it wasn't a bit like this,' she added. both of them knowing she was not talking about the weather.

'Thank goodness for that!' Jason said.

'Lord, Jason, my parents! They were only expecting me to be gone for a couple of hours.'

'How perfectly awful,' he mimicked her accent, and laughed. 'Now you'll have to marry me. Your father is probably deadly with a shotgun.'

'But what will they think? I must phone them and tell them . . . What am I going to tell them?'

'That I'm holding you to ransom,' he said with a twinkle. 'Oh, don't worry angel, I'll talk to them.'

'And how are you going to explain this?'

'I'm not. I'm the guy who believes in honesty, remember? I'll just tell them the truth. Only the truth.'

She slid her arms round him, holding him as he held her. Yes, she thought. the truth was something her parents would understand, and so would Leon. Her beautiful, teasing Jason had brought the laughter back into her life.